She was locked in the bedroom of a desolate Scottish castle—alone with the man she had sworn to destroy!

As Ian came toward her, she sought wildly for escape. There was none.

"I despise and detest you," she cried. "Does that attract you?"

"Immensely," he answered as his arms closed round her.

With a single movement, Ian tore her dress from neck to hem and he lifted her high in his arms. The firelight gleamed on the whiteness of her body, glittered on the gold of her tumbled hair.

She cried out, but there was no one to hear her. Triumphantly he carried her into the shadows of the great bed.

SWEET PUNISHMENT

Barbara Cartland

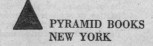

PYRAMID BOOKS
NEW YORK

Dedicated to
MARJORIE SOTHEBY
"Sympathy and Understanding—her jewels"

SWEET PUNISHMENT

A PYRAMID BOOK

Pyramid edition published February 1973

Copyright 1931 by Barbara Cartland

All Rights Reserved

ISBN 0-515-02920-3

Printed in the United States of America

Prologue

"DIANA! Diana!"

The sick man repeated his incessant cry, throwing out his arms and tossing off the scanty bedclothes from the roughly improvised bed on the sandy floor.

Softly a large figure moved through the door-way of the tent and soothed him again to silence, raising his head for a drink of water.

Outside, the native bearers lay exhausted after a hard day's march. The camp-fire was sinking low, for already the night was far spent. From the depths of the jungle around the camp came the sound of wild beasts seeking their prey, and the harsh yell of the jackals.

Inside the tent the sick man sank into a heavy slumber.

Quietly his attendant lowered himself to the rug which lay beside the bed, and dropped into the easy sleep of a man used to snatching his rest whatever the circumstances around him.

An hour later the African dawn flung its first pale light on the sleeper's faces. Ian Carstairs was sleeping with his head thrown back, one strong arm raised above his head.

He was a huge man of about six foot three. His body was in perfect condition, strong, lithe, and tanned almost mahogany colour by the tropical sun. He had the determined chin and strong features of a man who has always had his way, but his broad forehead gave promise of more than brute strength, and his mouth showed signs of humour.

His companion, even without the wasting effects of fever, was of far weaker physique. He had the imaginative, sensitive face of a dreamer. He was younger, too, only about twenty-five.

He stirred now restlessly, and opened his eyes slowly to consciousness.

It was only a light movement, but Ian rose from the floor and sprang quickly to his side. He brushed back the lank hair from the boy's forehead and moistened his parched lips.

"Feeling better?" he asked gently.

Jack Melbourne nodded.

"I can't go on again today," he whispered.

His voice was hoarse and as cracked as the bloodless lips through which it came.

"Nonsense," Ian replied. "We have only another fifty miles or so now, and the boys will carry you as carefully as possible."

Jack shook his head.

"No," he whispered, "I can't go on."

Outside the tent the black boys were already collecting together the stores they had unpacked the night before, and were preparing the rough litter on which they had carried the sick man for many weary miles.

Ian's expression was troubled as he watched them and noted the muttered, almost furtive conversation they were holding amongst themselves. He hesitated a moment, then squared his shoulders as if he faced something antagonistic.

He bent towards the sick man, and though his words were rough his voice was very gentle. "You've got to do it, Jack," he said.

"I can't, Ian—really I can't. I am going to die, and even you can't stop me."

Jack spoke with intensity, and the effort was too much for him. A fit of coughing racked his whole body,

6

sweat poured from his forehead, and he tried weakly to brush it from his eyes.

A final *rigor* shook him until he lay back utterly exhausted, his teeth chattering and his hands clenched feebly, as if to steady his self-control.

There was no doubt that he was a very ill man, and Ian Carstairs looked at him in silence, his face expressing only a little of the deep anxiety he felt.

The fifty miles or so he had spoken of were nearer two hundred: two hundred miles of hard walking before they could find civilization, and, what was more important, water. Food they had in plenty, but their water supply was running short.

Their progress had naturally been impeded by the necessity of carrying the sick man.

The jungle through which they had passed was comparatively easy to negotiate single file, but where men had to walk abreast with a little on their shoulders it often necessitated a certain amount of clearing.

Ian was facing that terrible problem, seeking vainly for a solution, when Jack's hand on his arm made him bend down hastily to catch the weak whisper.

"You can't do it, old man. Clear out and leave me. What is one life compared with nine?"

There was no answer. Ian dropped on his knees beside his friend, and for a moment hid his eyes with his hands.

The black boy whom Ian had put in charge of the others approached the entrance to the tent.

"It is time to go, master," he said.

Ian started to his feet and walked outside to speak to him apart.

"We can't go today, Joe," he said.

"We must, master." The black man spoke firmly. "We have enough water for only three days more, after that we go thirsty till we reach a settlement."

"We can't leave him," Ian said, pointing to the tent.

7

The black man said slowly:

"We must, master—there is no other way."

"Not if I have to carry him myself," Ian answered.

But as he spoke there came a sound that made them stiffen into a startled silence—the report of a revolver-shot. It shattered the still air, causing the native boys to spring to their feet. They hurried behind Ian to the door of the tent.

On the floor, where he had crawled from his bed, Jack lay. In his hand was a revolver; from his chest the blood was flowing swiftly on to the sand beneath him.

"Jack! Jack!"

In an agony Ian raised him in his arms.

The dying man tried to speak. Twice he attempted it, then at last, with a convulsive effort, just audible to Ian's hearing, came the words:

"Tell Diana I loved her."

Then blood spurted horribly from his mouth in a crimson stream, and he fell back dead.

Chapter 1

LADY DIANA STANLIER was without a doubt the most beautiful person in the room.

It was a dance given by a leading member of the young married set, and there were few girls present. But Diana was too beautiful, and too famous, not to be asked to every function, however large, or however small, in London society.

She was not very tall, but she had the Stanlier bearing, which her many forebears had made as famous as the history they had created.

She had golden hair with a touch of red in it, dark eyes, and an expressive mouth. At twenty-five, she was the most talked-of young woman in England.

Her beauty, which caused envy and admiration in the hearts of all women, was portrayed in most photographers' windows, hung on the walls of the Academy, and featured in every picture paper.

If there was a pageant, she was the Queen of Beauty. If there was a crusade, a charitable appeal, or a national protestation, Diana headed the list; if there was a race to be won, a flight to be made, or an experiment to be proved on road, on sea, or in the air, Diana was invariably the first to attempt, the first to achieve.

And she was rich, she was beautiful, and she was witty.

Naturally, she had admirers in plenty, but so far she had refused to marry any of them. Amuse her they could and did for a short while, but all too quickly she tired; and then an ardent suitor found the front door in Grosvenor Square closed against him.

Little wonder that, with the added background of an adoring father and a doting mother, Diana found life too easy. As a stimulant against so much sweetness she required excitement, and excitement she had to have, at whatever the cost.

Often she would seek it in escapades as stupid as the publicity the cheap newspapers gave them; but, the moment of exhilaration past, Diana herself found the aftermath as obnoxious and contemptible as did her severest critics.

Tonight, at the Veritys' dance, she had discovered a new amusement.

It promised to be only a momentary one, and, had Diana paused to think, she would have known the game was not only unworthy of her but also not worth the consequences which would inevitably attend its finality.

But she did not hesitate; as usual, the future would not concern her, until it became the present.

He, the new amusement, was a newly fledged member of Parliament, whose success in the constituency had completely turned his head.

Considering himself fascinating, he had bothered everyone until he finally achieved an introduction to Diana; and now, unconscious of the smiles his conceited posturings were causing, unaware that Diana, already warned, was leading him on, he preened himself and spread his peacock glory before her.

Out in the garden he pressed her hand and, emboldened by her acquiescence, asked if he might escort her home. Diana's acceptance delighted him, and he could not resist the temptation to mention the fact, too casually to be natural, to one or two acquaintances.

Of the subsequent events of the evening he afterwards remembered very little. It was a chaotic whirl of humiliation and pain.

He had, however, an unforgettable memory of Diana's scorn when he attempted to kiss her in the taxi, and several nasty bruises to remind him how, on arrival at her home, he had been seized by many joyous spirits who awaited them, who propelled him forcibly through the house, to fling him violently into a fountain in the garden.

With sodden garments and with chattering teeth he had fled from Grosvenor Square to his club, jeers and laughter echoing in his ears.

Ashamed and impotently furious, it would have been little consolation for him to have known that, suddenly bored with the whole affair, Diana had turned her friends abruptly from the house and gone wearily to bed.

In her bedroom she had stared for a long time at her reflection in the looking-glass. It was a very lovely self which looked at her.

In the white dress, which showed up her fair skin, she might indeed have stepped out of one of the Lawrence pictures which hung in the dining-room downstairs. But there was a frown between her eyes, and her red mouth was set in hard displeasure.

With an impatient movement she turned from the mirror. She took off her dress to slip into a dressing-gown, then she pulled up the blind and opened the window.

Her room looked over the Square. It was nearly dawn; and in the distance she could hear the rumble of lorries as they went hurrying towards Covent Garden with their loads of vegetables and flowers from the country.

The garden in the Square looked mysterious and blue in its quiet shadows. A taxi passed noisily, driving some belated reveller home, and a policeman paused on his beat to see if all doors were closed and barred.

Then, against the railings on the opposite side of the road, in the shadow of an over-hanging tree, she became conscious of a man's figure. He had been standing so still that she had not noticed him at first.

He was very tall, with unusually broad shoulders, and to her surprise he was staring up at the house. He wore a dinner-jacket, his hands were deep in the pockets of the coat, and he was hatless, as if, in spite of the unusual hour, he had just come out for a stroll.

As she moved, he raised his head and saw her, staring as if he were trying to identify her across the distance which divided them.

Then, when she drew back into the darkness of her room, he turned and walked slowly away. She watched him until he passed out of sight, but he did not look back.

Vaguely, Diana wondered who he was and why he was there. It was not the first time by any means that she had been silently serenaded.

Love-lorn young men had often watched disconsolately beneath her window; but she was certain, though she could hardly distinguish his features, that she had never seen this man before.

Somehow, quite unreasonably, he interested her. For a moment she had formulated the idea of going down to speak to him; then, laughing at herself, she drew down the blind, and, ten minutes later, she was fast asleep.

The morning brought her a consciousness that she had once again behaved not only badly but idiotically. She was sorry for the stupid young man who had received a needlessly hard punishment for presumption.

She suddenly felt sickened that she had allowed herself to be mixed up in what was nothing better than the thoughtless ragging of small schoolboys. Yet her pride would not allow her to own publicly to a fault, and when her mother reproached her she merely laughed in reply.

The Stanliers had always been proud; indeed, when

12

James the First had created the earldom, the head of the family had refused to accept it in any other name.

This, today, made the Stanlier lineage unique in the pages of Debrett, for the Earldom of Stanlier carried for the heir the courtesy title of Viscount Stanlier, and any other issue bore, too, only the name of Stanlier.

Diana was the only child of the present seventh Earl. Through much spoiling, in her the pride of her family had become perverted into hardness and indifference to others, which was almost callousness.

What had been a fine bravery in her great-grandfather, who had faced certain death with a smile, and had been courage in another Stanlier who had attacked when only retreat could have saved his life, was in Diana only a lack of true feeling and deep emotion.

She had no sympathy for weakness, and she despised people, especially women, who showed any evidences of it. But, having never faced anything more momentous in her own life than a decision of accepting or refusing a proposal of marriage, she was a poor companion, save for those joyous spirits who were living for the moment only.

She was lovely, she was intelligent, but no one had yet discovered her heart. Her family had long since given up trying to influence her where men were concerned.

Diana's impatience at any maternal advice as to the eligibility of suitors was obvious, and Lady Stanlier had to be content with the poor consolation of the ancient adage that there were "just as good fish in the sea . . ."

Diana was running downstairs, dressed for riding, when her mother met her in the hall.

"There is a Mr. Carstairs to see you, darling," she said. "He says it is important."

"Oh, damn! . . . Who is he? What does he want?"

Diana was in a bad mood this morning, and anything was likely to upset her.

"He insisted on seeing you," Lady Stanlier replied;

"but he seems very nice. I don't think I've met him before."

Diana stood still as she considered who this Carstairs could be. She was dressed in Jodhpurs and a pale-blue shirt; she had no accessories of hat or coat to impede her freedom of movement, only a small riding-whip in her ungloved hand.

No, she could not recall knowing anyone of that name. Perhaps it was the Press; she fervently hoped that last night's escapade had not already reached the ever-ready ears of the newspapers.

"It can't really be important," she said to her mother, and went into the library.

Standing on the hearthrug was one of the best-looking men she had ever seen. Vaguely he seemed familiar to her, but she could not remember where or when she had met him.

"How-do-you-do?"

He took her outstretched hand.

"I am sorry to stop your ride, Lady Diana," he said, "but I have a message for you. I am afraid I have been a long while in delivering it—in fact, over a year."

"A message for me?" Diana raised her eyebrows.

"From Jack Melbourne," he said.

Diana frowned.

"Jack Melbourne?" she echoed. "I cannot . . ."

She hesitated, then after a pause went on:

"Oh yes, I remember. I knew him several years ago. How is he? But why should he send me a message?"

A faint expression of anger crossed Ian's face when Diana said she could not remember Jack. All too vividly he could hear that ceaseless cry—"Diana! Diana!"

He saw again Jack's face when, in his last words, he mentioned the love which had tormented him and haunted his sleep night after night, when the fever was at its worst.

At that moment, Ian could willingly have killed Diana for her beauty which had caused such agony, and for

14

her flippancy about a man to whom she had meant so much. Sternly he answered her.

"Jack Melbourne is dead."

Just for a moment she was disconcerted. Then she said quietly, "I am sorry."

"He died," Ian said, "that his companions might not be hampered by his disability. He saved nine lives, including mine, by shooting himself. I have just returned from Africa, and my first duty on arrival is to tell you his last words, which were a message to you."

"Yes?"

Diana waited; her dark eyes were raised to him, but their expression was inscrutable, and Ian could not tell her thoughts.

"As he was dying he whispered: 'Tell Diana I loved her.'"

Unconsciously his voice softened on the words, but immediately afterwards it became grim as he added:

"I hope you now remember who he was."

Diana stiffened at the tone of his voice, filled with contempt. She was not used to men speaking to her so. Like a horse that suddenly feels the spur, she became alert, but she answered quietly:

"Of course, I remember now. When you first said his name you took me by surprise. I had not seen Jack for two years."

"I did not know," Ian said bitterly, "that it was so easy for a woman to forget a man who loved her."

"Perhaps you don't know anything about love," Diana answered.

"Not your kind," Ian replied.

For a moment they stood staring at each other. War was declared between them.

Ian, tall, bronzed, a product of outdoor life, a man in the true meaning of the word, unsophisticated, even primitive, yet withal sure of himself; Diana, the product of an over-civilized world, polished until the truth of her was lost under a veneer of artificiality,

15

lovely, desirable, yet with her real character disguised and hidden, even from herself.

As she faced him, Diana wanted him to bow before her in homage as other men had always done.

She wanted his subservience, and she was stung by his contempt, in much the same way as an Eastern queen might feel outraged at the impertinence of a slave.

And Ian, though furious with her, was at the same time conscious of her loveliness. With her head thrown back, her eyes blazing, her slim figure drawn up to its full height, she was unbelievably beautiful, but also she was an embodiment of the modern girl, of whom he had much to learn.

"How dare you be so rude?" Diana said furiously. "You presume to come here and insult me because I forget some tuppeny-halfpenny young man! As if I was likely to remember in a minute all the fools who have ever been in love with me! Jack Melbourne was a sloppy, lovesick idiot for whom I had no use—if he is dead, and out of this life, so much the better, without all your 'greater love' stuff. . . ."

"Stop!" Ian sprang forward and seized her wrist. "I won't have Jack spoken of like that! He was too fine for you to understand him—I see that! He is better dead, than in love with someone like you."

Both were afire with anger.

Diana strove to release her wrist from his strong clasp. Ian was hardly conscious that he held her, and for a brief second she struggled. The indignity broke her last vestige of control.

She raised her riding-whip and hit him across the face.

Chapter 2

A LONG red weal burnt itself across Ian's cheek; but he stood as if turned to stone, only his hands clenched slowly until the knuckles went bloodless under the tan.

As her moment of ungovernable temper passed, the blood rushed to Diana's face, then receded until she was deathly white. But her eyes never faltered; they challenged Ian and defied him.

What he would have said, what would have been their first movement, they never knew, for the door opened and Lord Stanlier entered the library.

"Ah, Diana, my dear," he said, "I did not know you were here."

Diana turned towards her father, as with old-world courtesy he immediately greeted Ian with outstretched hand.

"Mr. Carstairs, Father," she murmured reluctantly.

"How-do-you-do?" Lord Stanlier said, adding, "You must be Bobbie Carstairs' son."

"Yes, sir," Ian answered.

"Exactly like him, I should have known you anywhere—but surely you were in Africa? I remember hearing so when I read of his death three months ago."

"That's quite right, sir," Ian replied. "I was up country in a most inaccessible part, and only got the news a month afterwards. I came home as soon as I could—my first visit for five years."

"Too long, my boy! You must make up for it by letting us entertain you as much as possible. Your father was one of my oldest friends—even though he invariably beat me at bridge."

"Thank you, sir, but I have to go North tonight."

"To your island?" said Lord Stanlier. "I remember your father saying frequently that the family place was too isolated for him. However, you must lunch with us now. I will take no refusal."

Against his will, but finding it impossible to avoid the friendliness of Lord Stanlier, and ironically amused by Diana's sulky disapproval, Ian accepted.

For luncheon, Diana changed from her riding-breeches, which made her look charmingly boyish, into a dress of soft chiffon, which was very feminine, as it clung to her, revealing her perfect figure.

Her fair hair was drawn behind her ears to fall in a row of tiny curls at the nape of her neck, and she had darkened her eyelashes and painted her scornful mouth until it was crimson like the roses she wore at her waist.

As Lord and Lady Stanlier talked, interested in his adventures, asking him questions, Ian found himself watching Diana.

Once, at some reference to Jack, the colour flamed into her cheeks, and she raised angry eyes to his; and from that moment a strange cruelty foreign to his nature made him want to torment her so that, again and again, he drew her into the conversation, forcing her to reply to him.

She was like a wild, beautiful animal, he thought; at heart quite untamed by captivity, yet encoiled with luxury and flattery, until only on a rare occasion would she reveal her underlying fierceness.

She was all-woman in her seduction, in her physical perfection, but as yet utterly unawakened to any feminine gentleness of heart or soul.

When Lady Stanlier asked him how he had got the mark on his cheek, Diana smiled, a slow, sarcastic smile.

"Doubtless by a gallant action," she said, before Ian could answer.

Her tones were honey-sweet to deceive her parents; but Ian knew the underlying irony, and saw the malicious glint in her eyes.

"I'm afraid not," he answered lightly. "Only an unexpected encounter with something of no consequence."

Again Diana felt her temper rise, that this man, this primitive bore, should dare to ignore her.

She could not deny that he was good-looking, and she owned frankly to herself that in other circumstances his physical strength alone might have attracted her. But it was his seeming indifference which was infuriating her more every minute.

Had he been obviously angry, or even embarrassed, she could and would have coped with the situation, but she was now the more self-conscious of the two.

She had a terrible suspicion that he was only mocking her; and never before in her whole life had Diana, whatever the circumstances, been anything but supreme.

In the right or in the wrong, she had cast a man down or raised him again to happiness. One she had scorned might rage against her, but in itself that proved she had stirred a depth of uncontrollable emotion.

But this was something new, something unable to be borne, that a man should receive her insults with the amusement of an onlooker at the bad-tempered naughtiness of a spoilt child.

She felt that she hated Ian, that she would do anything to dominate him and prove her superiority.

Suddenly an idea came to her. She would prove her power by making this fool who disdained her pay the uttermost homage a man can pay. She would make him love her.

So often her friends had proclaimed her attractions, so often her charm had drawn seemingly impervious men to her feet, that Diana did not believe for a moment she could encounter failure where Ian was concerned.

All through her life men had fallen, almost too easily, in love with her; but sometimes she had deliberately tried to attract, and never had she failed in her objective.

She realized that Ian was not going to be an easy capture. She was clever enough and knowledgeable enough to know that where the woman he loved was concerned he would have a Victorian standard of propriety.

Yet she told herself that the victory would be all the greater, when he surrendered to her ultra-modern appearance and outlook.

Diana had few morals. She had not been a leader of London society for over five years without having views which were so tolerant and broad-minded that most people would have considered them loose.

Her friends preyed on one another, had few conventional barriers which they would not break down, and a code of honour which they could easily evade.

The men she knew borrowed money they could not return, made love to one another's wives, and did not disguise the fact that their intentions were strictly dishonourable.

Her woman friends were charming, but utterly unscrupulous where the capture of a young man was concerned.

They were happy enough in a vague, slipshod way, seeking amusement diligently; their only virtue the courage with which they faced the monetary ups and downs of their lives.

Amusement was the only thing which mattered to them: anyone, so long as he or she were amusing, was admitted to their society.

That was the only thing demanded, the only passport required, that a newcomer should be entertaining —"good value" was the expression generally used.

Where a generation ago a girl of Diana's position would have been guarded, chaperoned, and protected, Diana met all and sundry. Human nature, therefore, held few surprises for her.

She had no illusions and, sadly enough, no ideals. How could she, when she had known and appreciated every sort and type of man?

One night she would dine with someone of the oldest aristocracy; the next, she would find her dinner-partner in a cabaret artist, who had been born in the slums of Whitechapel.

And yet their conversation was curiously similar, for a man, be he of high or low degree, has but one attitude towards a young and beautiful girl.

Diana lived on love, and lived dangerously, but that was the only life she desired, the only entertainment which really amused her.

She cared for sport only from the point of view of who companioned her; it mattered little to her whether she spent the afternoon in a cinema beside a man whom she liked for the moment, or went driving with him in the bright sunshine.

She believed in her body, knowing only too well the power its beauty gave her. She had no other god but herself, and living the inane, hectic life which she did, there was nothing and no one to prove her wrong.

Now she would prove her power, prove the omnipotency of her gods.

Revenge, she had been told, was sweet; and she would taste it to the full when Ian, like other men, was hungry for her.

If she had but known, the way would have been so easy—she would have had no need to plan, no need to scheme.

Among Jack Melbourne's things Ian had found a photograph of Diana, a snapshot taken in the country. Diana, aged about nineteen, was standing in a garden with a fat setter puppy in her arms.

She was laughing into the camera, and the wind had swept the hair from her forehead and blown her skirts around her slim form. She looked very young and very happy, a typical example of a beautiful and healthy English girl.

Ian had put the photograph in his pocket, meaning to return it to the original when he met her. In those long days in the jungle he had found himself often looking at it.

It had made him curiously homesick for England, for the green countryside and the long, peaceful days with no lurking danger, and when the only noise would be the bees humming round the flowers.

In his lonely life he had often longed for the companionship of a woman.

He had known very few women well. His mother, whom he had idolized, had died when he was a small boy, but his memory of her was very real.

He remembered her soft voice and gentle dignity, the kisses she had given him, and the clinging of her arms when she bade him good night.

Indeed, so vivid in his mind was her beauty and charm that he had found, as he grew up, that he expected any woman he cared for to reach the high standard his childish remembrances had set for him.

And so, though he had laughed with, and enjoyed the society of, feminine acquaintances, not one had owned him or really drawn his love.

Sweet women, gay women, war-time girls desperately anxious to make those precious six days' leave into a riot of enjoyment—he had kissed them and forgotten them, and held only to his yet unfound ideal.

And on those scorching marches after Jack had died, he had thought of Diana so much that what he saw only as a pictured face had gradually become an invisible companion beside him.

He had talked to that companion, told her how much he wanted to achieve success on this expedition; told her how short the water was getting, how badly the black boys needed encouragement; told her that he himself was growing desperately tired.

When finally they had reached their objective he had found himself unable to leave immediately for England.

Another expedition was waiting, and he would not disappoint the authorities who were relying on him to obtain the information they desired.

Off again he had journeyed—into the forests, where no white man had been before; over marshes which were so dangerous that one false step meant instantaneous death; into swamps where fever lurked ready to grip its victim; and with him, as if it were a talisman, journeyed that photograph of Diana.

Once they had rested in a native village. The inhabitants were a fine, strong race, who had intermarried with Arabs and were not so dark as the usual African native.

Ian, who had found great favour with the Chief, and obtained from him an important concession in return for an assurance of British interest and support, found himself in a strange situation; for the chief presented him with one of his daughters.

She was a very beautiful girl of about fifteen, with the exquisite figure of early maturity, combined with the almost royal carriage which is the birthright of the African native.

She had wide, dark eyes in an oval face. She was naked save for a bead girdle, and her perfect little breasts, like the rest of her body, were not darker than the warm gold of burnished brass.

Ian had seen no white woman for over six months, and then only burnt-complexioned, heat-shrivelled wives of up-country officials; but the photograph in his pocket dismissed absolutely the slightest question of accepting this munificent gift.

It was no temptation, only a problem requiring tact.

23

In the dimness of his tent he had looked away from the bright eyes gazing adoringly at him; he had ignored, without any effort, the seduction of that beautiful golden body and the fluttering supplication of tiny hands.

Courteously he had thanked the Chief and refused his present, his excuse being so diplomatic that there could be no possibility of ill-feeling.

But the Chief, disappointed, had withdrawn, and Ian had spent a sleepless night tossing wearily on his bed.

Dawn had found him up and dressed writing the dry documentary evidence which, nevertheless, in its achievement brought him a step nearer home.

Facing Diana now, across the dining-room table, he thought how he had imagined that, some day, he would tell her how much her pictured self had meant to him.

But with the soft voices of her father and mother in his ears, with the atmosphere of well-trained servants and the trappings of luxury and wealth around him, he saw the impossibility of conveying in words even a semblance of a life where a man must cling to a strong anchor or drift into a vortex, from which there is no return.

How could he tell her of a loneliness so overwhelming that drink in its worst form is preferable; or of an isolation from everything familiar, which drives a man to association with fallen women and to the vicious evil of native witchcraft?

Even if she knew the beastliness of it, she could never feel the pity which attends true understanding of human limitations.

A man had died under the African sun, but Diana had danced his memory away; a man had believed in her, and it counted less than a merry jest; a man had dreamed of her, to find a disillusioned awakening.

Ian's fingers closed in his pocket on the worn and faded photograph, and suddenly he crushed it into many pieces.

Chapter 3

IAN had a grand welcome from his "ain folk".

The island of Ronsa lay at the extreme south of the Western Isles, and was divided from the mainland of Scotland only by a narrow channel.

The island was about twenty miles broad and consisted mostly of fine grouse land, the centre of the island rising several hundred feet, but sloping away on the north side to low marshes where the snipe were plentiful.

Castle Ronsa stood on high cliffs facing the Atlantic, the building itself framed by pines—the only trees on the island. Of grey stone, it was of a gaunt, grim appearance.

Stone turrets guarded each corner of the building, and a high centre tower made a fine look-out. The original foundations were centuries old; the complete building, however, being mostly of the seventeenth century.

Battles had been planned in this stronghold and a Royal fugitive sheltered, but the generations of Carstairs following the failure of young Charles Stuart had found the peacefulness of Scottish politics too tame, and had spent most of their lives in the South.

However, Ian's grandfather, on his inheritance, had made his home here, and had reigned royally for more than sixty years over the few inhabitants of the island.

He had returned to ancient custom and made the

island almost self-supporting, scorning to obtain provisions from the mainland. The crofters adored him, and Ian's father had been a great disappointment to them when he preferred to live in England.

Few of them could speak English; Ian's grandfather, the old Laird, had never spoken anything but Gaelic, even to his son.

The crofters of Ronsa seldom visited the mainland; like a huge family, for—though maybe distantly—they were all related to one another, they were a superstitious people, and dour to all but their own kin.

Ian's father had alienated himself from them and they hated him, becoming silent and lowering in his presence, so it was little wonder that towards the end of his life the Castle was closed.

After his mother's death, until his grandfather died, Ian had lived at Ronsa, for his father had found the upbringing of a small boy too much trouble.

Ian loved every moment he spent on the island, and the "wee Laird", as the crofters called him, was adored in return by every one of them.

There was not a cottage where he was not welcome, and before he was six years old he knew every man, woman, and child by name; and, later, his grandfather saw to it that he knew their history as well.

The old Laird studied his people. There was no need for lawyers on Ronsa; every argument and every quarrel was brought to him for settlement, and he dealt them justice.

They were a primitive people and primitive methods suited them—a quarrel was more often than not settled by the use of fists, with the Laird himself as referee. But whatever his judgment, they abided by it; they respected him.

Indeed, their feelings came very near to reverence, and his word was law until the day of his death.

He died in the middle of the war, and Ian, who had obtained special leave for the funeral, never forgot the strange, if awe-inspiring, sight. Ian's father was ill and unable to be present, and Ian was the sole representative of the family.

The old man had left special instructions, and they were obeyed.

Ronsa is a long journey from France, and Ian arrived the morning of the funeral; already the whole island had "viewed the remains", and they only awaited his appearance to begin the burial itself.

It was a bright September morning. The sea was emerald in the sunshine, and the distant peaks of Skye were veiled in a blue mist. The heather was in bloom and the grouse were calling on the moor.

Ian crossed from the mainland in a motor-boat, and as he came within sight of the Castle he saw that a great company of people were waiting at the entrance; the flag on the tower was at half-mast, and every window in the house shuttered and barred.

He stepped ashore; no one greeted him; he walked in silence and alone up the pathway; then the crowd parted for him to pass through the great, nail-studded door which was swung open on its ancient wrought-iron hinges, and he walked slowly, with bared head, into the huge baronial hall.

In the dimness he saw there the bier, and on it his grandfather. The body was in full Highland dress with the hands, crossed on the claymore, lying on his breast.

For a minute or so Ian stood there, saying a silent farewell to an old man whom he had loved; then came the skirl of the pipes, and the bearers filed slowly out of the hall.

The pipes led the way, following the bier, Ian walking behind; after him the crowd, the women in tears, the men with bowed heads.

Up the valley towards the hill, the long procession wound its way through the heather, the pipes never ceasing their lament. On the summit stood an unlighted beacon, at its foot a deep grave lined with heather.

27

Without a coffin, into the bare land he had loved so much, the old Laird was laid in his last sleep.

There was no service, no spoken prayers, save in the hearts of those he had served, as they had served him. The pipes voiced the sorrow of all; the waves below, surrounding them on every side, moaned in sympathy.

Ian, as was his right, crumbled the first handful of earth over the grave, after the sweet heather had covered the body.

Then, when the ground was level to the grave, each and all brought and laid a large grey stone, until over the resting-place of their Laird they had built a huge cairn.

The beacon was lighted, and the tune of the pipes changed into a song of triumph, a hymn of life. "The soul is not dead, it lives."

The melody swelled louder and louder, as the flames leapt higher, then in a final burst of impassioned sound came the marching song of the Highlanders, and the procession was led homewards.

Once more at the Castle, they turned in silence to face the hill. Beside the cairn, the beacon burned brightly, telling its message of hope.

The sunshine, brilliant and golden, from a deep-blue sky, was on the purple heather, the red stag-grass, the fields in the valley below, where the barley was ripening, and on the waves as they broke iridescent on the shore.

The island seemed a fitting grave for a great man. There was not a soul among the crowd who did not individually remember his kindness, his tolerance, and his generosity. There was not a dry eye as they stood, their black clothes a strange contrast to the wonderful colours around.

Then Ian spoke.

"God rest him," he cried in Gaelic, and a deep sound broke from those around him—an amen which needed no words to convey its sincerity.

Then, without further ado, they entered the Castle, where the funeral meats awaited them.

After his father inherited, Ian seldom visited the island, for Colonel Carstairs was jealous of his son's popularity. So when the war was over, he came back only at rare intervals, and then he sailed for Africa, and Ronsa saw him not for many years.

But the people did not forget him, and they welcomed him now with open arms and loosened tongues.

After greeting many friends of his boyhood, who drank his health in their own pot-still whisky, he had a long talk with the factor of the estate.

The moor was in good condition, the grouse rather over-stocked, as they had not been shot for several seasons, the home farms were paying their way and the tenants were contented.

Ian had come to a goodly heritage, and his gratitude went out to those who had kept things together during the years of his father's neglect.

The castle required only electric light to modernize it. In good repair and beautifully furnished, it was comfortable as well as magnificent.

The great Baronial Hall in the centre of the building reached to the roof and was hung with a rare collection of dirks and ancient claymores. The Dining-room overlooking the Atlantic was panelled with strange carvings, done by the island carpenters in bygone years.

Upstairs, the enormous State Bedroom held the great tapestry-hung four-poster bed, where generations of Carstairs had been born, and where Charles Stuart had once slept.

Ian, however, chose a smaller room for his own, a bright room with windows facing both the sea and the pine trees. To the east of the Castle was flat pasture-land where, Ian saw, one could land an aeroplane with ease.

The old Laird had bred many fine horses, which

he had sold for large sums; in fact, the Ronsa breed was quite famous.

The old man had been extraordinarily thrifty, and besides his quite considerable income he continually made money in different ways.

He was Scottish enough to love a bargain, yet wise enough to put back capital into furthering his schemes, so that Ian found, in spite of the interval of neglect, he had inherited a good stud and several small but prosperous local industries.

His heart rejoiced at the sport to be enjoyed, but he also vowed that his grandfather's enterprise should be continued and carried on, and that he would atone to the people for his father's indifference.

Here was his home, and here now, the wandering years forgotten, he intended to live and work. He realized, however, that he could not cut himself off entirely from the world—the life of the old Laird was not compatible with present-day conditions.

He at once ordered a motor-car, and investigated the different makes of airplanes.

The days after Ian's arrival were spent visiting his tenants, riding from house to house on a fine chestnut mare. At tea-time of the third day he found himself at the far end of the estate.

A large farmhouse lay under the lee of the hill, and Ian rode up to the door, dismounted, and knocked. He remembered Jock Ross well, a fine character and a good farmer. As he waited at the door, Ian could see the barns of well-stacked hay and the fat cattle in the fields near by.

In the farmyard, ducks were searching for food, and the open stable doors showed a glimpse of plough-horses resting after the day's labour.

Suddenly there was a sound inside the house, a chain was dropped abruptly and the key creaked in the heavy lock. The door swung open and a girl stood there.

"Good afternoon," Ian said in Gaelic. "Is Mr. Ross at home?"

To his surprise he was answered in English.

"Good day, Mr. Carstairs. My father will be back for tea. Will you come in?"

"Your father? Then you must be Jean," said Ian, holding out his hand, and receiving a smile of delight at his memory.

"It's clever of you to know me. Come away in."

Ian entered the house. He remembered years ago a thin, long-legged child who had out-run him at games and led him into all sorts of escapades for which he generally received the punishment.

In later years she had grown plumper, but was still ungainly with the strange proportions of a young foal. He had not expected to find she had grown up into a good-looking woman.

"You speak English, Jean—that is unusual here," he remarked, as he followed her into the small, stuffy parlour.

"I have been to Edinburgh University since we last met," she answered.

When she smiled, Ian decided she was almost beautiful. She was tall, with the full figure and broad shoulders of a country girl who has known manual labour since childhood, but she had red hair which flamed in tiny curls against a white skin which many an acknowledged London beauty would have envied.

She had large eyes and a generous mouth, naturally red and inviting. She was a surprising person, indeed, to have blossomed from a snub-nosed freckled child with skinny, carroty plaits.

"I should not have known you elsewhere, Jean," said Ian.

"You're not altered," she answered quietly, and Ian was silent, an incident of the past recurring to his memory.

He had been going back to school, and they had spent

the day together on the moor. Their luncheon of sandwiches had been consumed as they lay in the heather, and then they had wandered and played the whole afternoon, until dusk brought them back.

At the Castle gate, Jean had retrieved her bicycle from the hedge preparatory to riding home; then they shook hands solemnly in farewell.

"I wish you weren't going, Ian," Jean had sighed.

"So do I," Ian had answered, then had added hastily: "You're fine for a girl, Jean! When I grow up I'll take you round the world."

And Jean, in answer, had flung an arm about his neck and kissed him affectionately.

"Good-bye," she had said with a suspicion of a sob, and before her tears could shame her had ridden away down the dusty lane.

There were other incidents which Ian now remembered, moments when they had rolled in the heather, helpless with laughter, moments of fear when the old Laird had to be told of misdeeds . . . then, later, a moment of tears—he had come back to Ronsa to say farewell to his grandfather and his island friends before leaving for the front.

Most of the most important tenants had journeyed to the Castle to wish him "God-speed", Jean Ross and her father and mother amongst them.

The old Laird had received them, Ian by his side, rather self-conscious in his new uniform. After a little speech, Ian had started to shake hands all round, but when he reached Jean she had given a sudden cry and rushed from the room in tears.

In the silence between them now, Ian felt embarrassed by his memories, and he was relieved to hear the loud voice of Jock Ross outside in the farmyard.

"I'll fetch Father," Jean said.

She left the room hurriedly, avoiding Ian's eyes as though she, too, were shy.

Over a pot of tea and piles of hot scones, Ian

listened to the local gossip from Mrs. Ross, a fat, cheerful body, who could make a thrilling mystery out of the most commonplace occurrence.

Farmer Ross joined in the conversation, but Jean remained silent, her eyes downcast, save when she rose to replenish the plates or to fetch more hot water from the kitchen.

Only when Ian was ready to depart did she speak directly to him, saying:

"You will come again?"

"Of course," Ian answered with a laugh, "if Mrs. Ross can afford to be eaten out of house and home. I can't resist her scones!"

"Go along with ye!" cried the delighted Mrs. Ross.

But Jean did not laugh, and Ian, as he rode home, wondered a little at the sombreness of her expression as he had bade her good-bye.

Chapter 4

A WEEK later Diana waited in smiling anticipation for Ian to arrive and take her out to dinner.

Before her looking-glass she noted with satisfaction how her dress, green as a stream in the sunlight, fitted her slim body. Diamonds glittered in her ears and wide bracelets framed her wrists.

She knew that she was beautiful, and gloried in the fact that it had procured for her tonight a minor victory towards her final conquering of Ian.

Before he had left the house that first day, she had

been clever enough, and actress enough, to convince him that the apology she offered was sincere.

Ian could not doubt that she was utterly ashamed and that the contrite words which fell from her lips were as ingenuous as her eyes, which he thought glistened with the suspicion of a tear.

And later, after his arrival in Scotland, he had received a letter from her, begging that they should meet again and talk quietly about Jack; Diana had even hinted at a memorial to the dead man.

Ian could not refuse her request, and so he had arranged that they should dine together.

A man who was used to primitive people and primitive passions, he was prepared to forget Diana's outburst of temper.

He was also half intrigued to find out if the true Diana whom Jack had loved, and whom he himself had visualized from her photograph, was indeed a myth or but disguised by a social veneer.

Contented with her appearance, Diana sat down on the bed and picked up the telephone. She rang up Rosemary Makines, a great friend of hers.

Rosemary had been married for three years. She, also, was one of the beauties of London society, but she did not have the publicity which Diana had.

She had married Henry Makines for love, but soon found that love did not pay their bills or provide them with anything but a subject for incessant rows, so after a year's struggle to make two ends meet she had taken up journalism and become great friends with Lord Leadhold.

With his support, the Leadhold newspapers seldom went to Press without an article by "the beautiful Mrs. Makines, leader of our younger married set". Mrs. Makines for a few guineas was prepared to advise the British public on health, beauty, food, love, children, or in fact on any subject.

Lord Leadhold was, also, sufficiently interested to

find and support Henry Makines in a constituency in the North, which frequently required his presence.

Rosemary was still fond of her husband in a vague, undemonstrative way, but she found the temptation of a life unharassed by debt too comfortable to resist. Henry, spinelessly ignoring the obviousness of the situation, on every possible occasion defended and praised Lord Leadhold.

Society being slack of principle, and uninterested in Henry, did not ostracize him, merely abusing him behind his back.

Rosemary hurried to the telephone when she was told Diana wanted to speak to her.

"Is that you, darling?" she asked in her charming drawl.

"I had to ring you up," Diana answered, "to tell you I am just going out with Ian Carstairs."

"With our jungle friend?" said Rosemary, who had heard a full account of Ian. "What fun, darling! Do you think you will really make him fall in love with you? I'm sure he regards you as a Scarlet Woman!"

"He does!" Diana replied grimly. "But he has got to take his punishment, if it takes me a year."

Rosemary laughed.

"Oh, you will get him before that, my dear, unless he has a dusky wife and a family hidden somewhere. In that case, he will be eternally faithful—I know the type!"

"No, he is far too inhuman," said Diana, adding: "That reminds me—how is the old boy?"—referring to Lord Leadhold.

"As devoted as ever, thank goodness," answered Rosemary; "but Henry returns tonight."

"Well, think of me, being the innocent girl who has been misunderstood," laughed Diana, and after a few more words rang off.

In spite of her protestations, even to herself, she was interested in Ian apart from her crusade of revenge.

She could not help comparing his fine physique with that of the other men she was amusing herself with—James Reynolds, an entertaining companion, but who fussed over his food, complaining of indigestion; Monty Richards, who hated any sport but dancing; Roy Gremling, very beautiful, who was too lazy even to attempt to entertain her; and young Lord Rankin, who was only five feet five, and who was invariably laid up with influenza when she most needed him.

Diana had received more proposals than she could count; but though she flirted with her admirers, she could never bring herself to the point of accepting them.

Deep down in her heart, hidden by the hardness she had compelled herself into feeling and showing, Diana had a romantic dream which refused to be quite annihilated—she wanted to fall in love.

She thought she had thrown away her belief in love, with her belief in God and with her ideals, but one soft spot remained which she could not eradicate.

The princes in her childish fairy-tales, the heroes in the flapper novels she had loved, her own fundamental sweetness, kept alive that one beautiful thing, despite the scoffing sophistication of her world.

It was not entirely Diana's fault that she was cynical. She had "come out" at eighteen, incredibly lovely, very young and impressionable.

Her father and mother were foolish enough to allow her to join a set led by a cousin who was six years older—young married women who were bored with their husbands, girls of twenty-five and more who wanted only to amuse themselves, companioned by most of the young wasters of London, and Diana found herself laughed at, teased, and bullied into behaving as they did.

She discovered that men who made passionate love to her in the evening would excuse themselves next day on the plea of too much drink. Her first kiss, momentous enough to her, she gave to a man who, a week later, was cited as co-respondent in a notorious divorce case.

Once she listened, and nearly surrendered, to the impassioned pleading of a married man, only to find that he intended their love to be an underhand, clandestine affair, while he remained publicly faithful to his rich wife.

Disillusionment was naturally not long in coming to her. She became callous, taking no more than a surface impression of anyone, remaining entirely unmoved.

Inevitably, when her beauty brought her spectacular triumph, she was spoilt by the applause. Her character was strong enough for her to despise her companions, but not determined enough to make her leave them.

The more indifferent she became, the more they sought her out, praising and lauding her, making her so sure of herself that her conceit would have been intolerable had it been less justified.

Hidden within her was the child who cried because her beautiful toys were broken; outwardly, a disdainful young woman condescended to find amusement in the forced gaiety of fools.

To one person only was Diana natural, unchanged, invariably sweet, and that was her old nurse. Ellen had looked after her since she was a baby in arms.

Very old now, and crippled by rheumatism, she hardly ever left her room at the top of the house, but never a day passed with Diana visiting her. She alone knew the Diana who outwardly had long since vanished.

Ellen had lived for Diana for so many years that now she seldom thought of anyone but her. All day in her tiny room she would sew with enlarged knuckles and stiff fingers at delicate garments for Diana to wear. In the evening, she would sit listening anxiously for the light step on the stairs which foretold Diana's appearance.

Radiant and flushed with some success or other, Diana would burst into the room, talk vivaciously for

37

perhaps ten minutes, then go as quickly as she had appeared, but leaving behind a contented, happy old woman.

Tonight, after her telephone conversation, with still a few minutes to spare before Ian's arrival, Diana, holding up her long chiffon skirt, ran up to Ellen's room, bringing with her a faint smell of scent and powder, and making a lovely picture for Ellen to remember in later hours, which were often sleepless with pain.

"Who are you going out with tonight, my dearest?" Ellen asked.

She took an intense interest in all Diana's young men, liking this one, scorning another, but finding none good enough for her darling.

"Ian Carstairs," Diana answered; "the explorer I told you about."

"Ah, I remember," Ellen replied. "He sounds a fine man, my pet, better than all these other young nincompoops."

Ellen had a fine contempt for the pale-faced weak-physiqued escorts whom Diana occasionally brought to be interviewed by her.

"He's a brute, Ellen!" Diana cried. "Don't you dare to stick up for him."

She knew how easily Ellen would form an opinion about someone, generally perversely opposite to her own, and once her admiration was assured, Diana knew she would never hear the end of the lucky man's praises.

Ellen could be as obstinate as Diana herself; in fact, Lady Stanlier had often sighed and complained that Diana owed as much of her character to Ellen's example as to parental heredity.

"I'd like to see this Mr. Carstairs," Ellen said slowly.

"Nonsense, darling," Diana answered. "You always find fault with any men I produce, and I am certainly not going to bring this one upstairs for your disapproval."

"I'd like to see him," Ellen answered determinedly. "Please, dearie—you know how happy it makes me to meet your friends."

Diana weakened. She never could resist Ellen's appeals.

"You are an old nuisance," she said, kissing her warmly, "and you won't like him, but if you must judge for yourself, you must, I suppose. I'll go and see if he's arrived."

There was no one in the hall, but as she walked down the stairs the front-door bell rang, and she came slowly down the last steps to greet Ian.

She was posed against a huge stained-glass window which was on one side of the hall, and for a moment it seemed to Ian as if she were part of the window.

Her fair hair, with the light behind it, was like a halo round her head, her long, clinging dress seemed to take the folds of a medieval robe; she was in that second very unlike the unpleasant impression he held of her in his mind since their last meeting.

But when she spoke, the illusion of saintliness vanished, for she greeted him gaily, a faint, mischievous twinkle in her eyes.

"Much against his will, yet nevertheless he has come," she mocked.

"On the contrary," Ian contradicted her; "I am very glad to see you."

She told him briefly that Ellen wanted to meet him, explaining who Ellen was. "It is almost a royal command," she ended.

"Then of course it must be obeyed," Ian said, following her to Ellen's room.

Most young men behaved a little awkwardly after they had shaken hands with Ellen. There was very little to say to someone nearly bedridden, someone with whom they had no common topic of conversation; and they were also a little uneasy under Ellen's searching glance and the obvious seriousness with which she contemplated them, generally—and they knew it—finding them wanting where Diana was concerned.

But, a little to Diana's surprise, Ian not only found plenty to say but immediately drew Ellen out, so that she entered into quite a spirited yet friendly argument with him.

So interested were they in each other that Diana, quite unnecessarily, felt a little piqued, as if she were left out of things. She was accustomed to having Ellen's entire attention.

Abruptly she made a movement of departure, and as Ian rose, quite reluctantly, she flounced into the passage without saying good-bye. But Ellen's quavering voice called her back into the room.

"Aren't you going to say good night, my pet?" she asked a little wistfully.

And as Diana, repentant, bent down to kiss her, she whispered in her ear:

"He's a fine man, dearie—I like him."

Diana said nothing, but as she reached the door she looked back at her old nurse and, making her a little grimace, she said:

"You think you're a fine judge, but this time you're wrong!"

Then with Ian by her side she left the house and entered the waiting car.

Chapter 5

DIANA had chosen to dine at the Embassy Club, partly because she always enjoyed herself there, and partly from a childish desire to show off in front of Ian.

Most of her friends would be present, and for a woman to know three-quarters of the people in a room gives her confidence, and what she considers a suitable background for her beauty.

They were led to the best table, which, whatever restaurant she patronized, was invariably reserved for Diana. She waved to several acquaintances, speaking to two or three in her passage across the room, and no sooner were they seated than more friends came over to talk to them.

Diana introduced Ian, who was received with undisguisedly curious glances. Diana's retinue was too well known for a stranger not to cause surprise.

At last, when they were settled and their dinner ordered, Diana suddenly realized that conversation might be a little difficult. She was used to chattering inanities, but inanities which consisted of local gossip and of people with whom everyone she knew was familiar.

To be with a stranger who knew nothing of her world and nothing of her friends, made her for a moment recall the days when she first made her debut. Then she smiled at Ian, and said:

"What shall we talk about?"

Ian smiled in return.

"In other words, how shall I amuse you?" he said.

"If you can," Diana answered quickly.

"I am not boasting," he said. "I am only too conscious that we belong to different worlds."

"And mine is a shallow one," Diana added.

To her surprise, Ian took her seriously.

"Well, isn't it?" he asked.

"We can't all be explorers and do great deeds on the outposts of the Empire," she said sarcastically.

"No—only send people there," Ian replied quickly.

For a moment she flashed him an angry look, hating him but a moment later, remembering herself and her chosen part, she gave him a sweet smile and said gently.

"Won't you tell me about Jack?"

Ian started the story simply and baldly, but soon, carried away by his theme, it became a poignant tale dramatically told, so that Diana, in spite of herself, was carried away into imagining vividly enough the circumstances of Ian's narrative.

He told her how Jack Melbourne had come to him in Africa and offered his services in an expedition up-country. Ian had not hesitated to describe the dangers he would have to endure, but Jack had insisted that it was the life he desired.

"At first," Ian said, "he never mentioned you, and then when we became friends he told me how much he adored you, and how for years he had hoped he had a chance, however slender. Then gradually he had realized he was only being a nuisance to you, and, with what seemed to me to be extraordinary determination in one who rather lacked stability, he resolved to end the torture which he had been suffering. He paused then continued.

"He came to Africa, because, I suppose, he was young and impressionable enough to be true to the tradition that anyone who wishes to forget finds solace

there. I am only surprised he did not try the stereotyped big-game shooting.

"At first I thought he was a weakling, but his true
stamina was revealed. Physically he was not strong,
but he was good-humoured and cheerful, however he
felt. We endured discomforts under which most men
would have found their spirits damped and their resolution wavering—I was used to it, but Jack was not.

He fell ill, and he suffered all the minor tortures
which a man, who has grown soft with civilization,
finds when he first attempts to adventure. Jack smiled
through it all. He even encouraged us—me, who had
gone through it a hundred times, and black boys who
were born to such a life.

And all this time, remember, he was homesick with
an intensity which even I could not understand.

"I have never loved a woman as Jack loved you, and
always with him was that want, that ceaseless, aching
loneliness which only you could have assuaged. He de-
ceived us so completely that only when he at last collapsed with fever did his delirium tell me what an
unhealed sore his cheerfulness had hidden.

Then, when day after day, hour after hour, all
through the night, he cried for you, did I understand
how completely a beautiful woman can wreck a man
who loves her. Of his death I have told you before,
and of his heroic sacrifice that the rest of us might live."

Ian ceased speaking, and for a moment Diana felt
herself to be in that scorchingly hot, treacherous African jungle.

It was almost with surprise that she realized that the
band was still playing, men and women were moving
rhythmically around the room, that she was sitting on
a sofa with food before her and champagne in her
glass—food and drink she did not need, while men and
women in the world went hungry for bread and thirsty
for want of water.

Then Ian's set face, for he also had been upset in

43

the repetition of his story, recalled her thoughts to herself. This man despised her—blamed her for Jack's death.

Just for a moment she felt a sudden urge to excuse herself, to tell Ian it was not her fault that Jack had fallen so terribly in love with her.

Some men she had deliberately enticed, but not Jack. She had met him accidentally several times, and then, before she was aware that he had regarded her especially, he declared his love, and she had at once refused him, quite gently but firmly.

Afterwards he had certainly become a nuisance. He was madly jealous, and young enough to show it. When she was not with him he was miserable; when she was, he made scenes.

The climax had come when Jack had insulted someone she was with, someone she was fond enough of to resent their being dragged into an awkward situation. Diana had turned on Jack with a flash of the Stanlier temper, which she so often found uncontrollable.

She had told him definitely that she had no use and no affection for him; she commanded him to leave her and not to come near her again.

A week later, surprised at Jack's absence and in a way missing his continual telephone calls, she had heard he had left for abroad. Though at first she had wondered what had become of him, she later forgot his existence.

In fact, when Ian had arrived with his story that momentous morning, it was the first time she had heard Jack's name mentioned for over a year.

But her pride would not allow her to be weak even for a moment where Ian was concerned. He had insulted her, and her blood could not forget or forgive until revenge wiped out the stain.

That she had insulted him in return did not count. The Stanlier temper had been famous for generations.

Her great-grandfather had killed a man who had sneered at him.

His father before him had won a colony for England because someone had scoffed at the luxuriousness of his existence at home.

Diana was a throw-back. At heart she was as primitive as the black natives Ian had commanded so recently. But neither of them knew this, and her delicate white hands, with crimson-painted nails, so very symbolic of a soft civilization, lay on the table beside his, tanned and scarred.

So, after a moment of silence, Diana had changed the subject altogether; but in spite of her hauteur, Ian received the impression that his words had not fallen unheeded.

Then they had talked of many things, commonplace enough; but there was an undercurrent, for they were both intensely aware of each other. And when at last Diana had risen, for the place was emptying, Ian said:

"Would you hate to come for a drive? It is not cold, and I find I cannot sleep well in London. Walls seem to close me in and stifle me."

He was surprised at himself even as he spoke, for he had no intention of extending such an invitation; and Diana accepted charmingly.

It was a warm night, with just a few stars in the purple sky. Ian opened his car, and a few minutes later they were driving down Piccadilly, deserted except for a taxi or two and the dark, familiar figures huddled in search of sleep on the wooden seats and against the railings of the Green Park.

Gradually the street lights were fewer and fewer, until they were vanquished by trees and hedges.

Diana felt suddenly elated by the night and the speed. Her hair was blowing back from her face, and she loved the roughness of the wind.

She was conscious all the time of Ian at her side; of his fine, clear-cut profile; of his strong hands holding the wheel. She was curious about him, and although she had already decided that she hated and despised him, she had a strong feeling which she had never experienced before—that she did not entirely comprehend this man.

Diana had known so many men that she was absolutely convinced of their inability to surprise her. After a few hours of a man's company, whoever or whatever he was, she felt that she knew all about him, and could almost anticipate every move he would make in the game of flirtation.

When Ian had invited her on this drive she thought it was the usual one she had taken so often before, wandering out of London on warm summer nights, to linger by the riverside or under the shadow of some great tree, lured and lazily amused by the love-making of her escort, until dawn, coming all too quickly, would hurry them back to the city.

Tonight, however, there was no atmosphere of flirtation. Indeed, Ian seemed almost oblivious of her presence. He was frowning a little, in obvious concentration. Feminine-like, she instantly desired his attention; but she did not speak, and he remained abstracted.

She would make him, sooner or later, sorry for his negligence, she told herself savagely.

On and on they drove, their headlights golden on the dark roads, until slowly a moon came out from the clouds, throwing a silver light on everything, and then at last, they were alone on the deserted countryside.

Ian slowed down and stopped. He switched off the engine, and there was a silence between them and around them.

"Will you have a cigarette?" he said at length.

Diana took one out of his proffered case. He lit it for her, and she raised her eyes in the match-light—instinctively using an old trick which had never yet failed to draw attention to her beauty.

46

But Ian did not respond, and so at last in desperation Diana's hand was forced, and she made the opening move in what she termed the "game".

"Why so serious?" she asked gently.

"Was I? I'm sorry," Ian replied lightly. "I am used to being alone, and when I'm not, I forget my manners. Forgive me for boring you!" he added with a laugh.

"On the contrary," Diana said, "you interest me."

"I am glad," Ian replied. "Yes see, you interest me too."

Diana smiled a little smile of triumph to herself.

For a moment the night had bewitched him, and Diana was being so sweet, so unexpectedly charming, that he contemplated telling her about her photograph, and how she had captured and inspired his imagination. But perhaps Scottish caution prevented him, or maybe it was only the natural shyness of an undemonstrative man.

Anyway, the opportunity passed, and he let it, changing the subject with a question about Ellen, and Diana, who was not hampered by diffidence, told him a little of her childhood.

She tried to make the story of being an only child pathetic, and she succeeded. For in reality, though she herself was quite unaware of it, the story was a sad one.

All only children are to be pitied, unless their parents are wise enough to send them to school, where they find playmates and the broadening education of unselfishness.

But Diana's parents had considered her far too precious to subject her to the rough and tumble of any school, and therefore, brought up and companioned entirely by adoring grown-ups, she had never learned the joy of sharing or the lesson of self-restraint.

Little wonder now that she had no interests which did not directly concern herself.

Ian, listening to her tale of childish loneliness, understood how utterly indulgence, combined with her unusual beauty, had formed—or, rather, deformed—her character, until her whole outlook began and ended with herself.

Ian also had been an only child, but the loss of his mother, and his school life, had eliminated all spoiling, until he had reached almost the other extreme, to find a life nearly barren of deep affection.

"And so, you see," Diana concluded, thinking that she read in Ian's attention the success due to her wistful pose, "how lonely I have always been."

"Until you grew up," Ian corrected.

"Of course, not now," Diana answered; "I have so many friends. But still, sometimes . . ." a sigh completed the sentence.

Ian, remembering the collection of friends Diana had introduced to him at the Embassy, could understand that "sometimes", even while he was wise enough to guess that Diana herself was only pretending.

They gushed at Diana insincerely, while criticizing her actions unmercifully when she was out of earshot, maliciously repeating and exaggerating.

He wondered if Diana would ever have any conception of how wonderful a thing real friendship might be.

They talked for perhaps an hour, and then, without one intimate word, look, or gesture, without so much—Diana told herself afterwards—as a compliment, he switched on the engine and drove her back to her house.

It was a new experience, a surprising one. On the doorstep she held out her hand, and for the moment she was entirely genuine, as she said!

"I want to see you again."

Chapter 6

RONALD STEWART was jealous. For three months before Ian's advent to London he had been Diana's favourite.

He even thought of himself in that way, and though in his heart of hearts he had little hope of ever attaining a higher position, he had enjoyed his brief victory over the other supplicants.

He was very good-looking in a rather dark, slightly foppish manner, and Diana found him amusing—anyway, as a companion for luncheons and dinners.

Now Ronald found himself utterly deposed by the "jungle chief", as Diana's crowd had nicknamed Ian.

Never before had Diana been seen so little in the company of her own particular set. Even Rosemary hardly saw her, or heard from her, these days. Excepting for a week when Ian had returned to Scotland, she spent all her time with him.

"What she can see in the fellow, I don't know," Ronald said to Rosemary.

"He hasn't got much money, and certainly no conversation," Rosemary replied. "I never thought he would last more than a week or so."

They were having supper together, and even as they were talking, Diana and Ian entered the room. Diana was looking exceedingly lovely, and Ian seemed the perfect foil for her beauty. She was so fair and short and he so huge and bronzed. Although he was large, there was no clumsiness about him; but in the tawdry finery of a night club, he did indeed appear to be out of place.

The band was blaring and shrieking music which a primitive would have found unmelodious. Couples were swaying together in amorous embrace, their faces flushed either from drink or the closeness of the atmosphere; there was hardly any ventilation in what originally had been an underground cellar.

Pale-faced waiters were hurrying backwards and forwards with champagne and the breakfast dishes of kippers and eggs, which London society consumes for supper, the simplicity contrasting piquantly with the rich dinners they had enjoyed a few hours before.

Young girls were dancing extravagantly with men old enough to be their fathers; fat, over-jewelled women were breathing heavily on the arms of seedy gigolos.

This was life, this was enjoyment, this was so-called pleasure.

Presently a cabaret of lewd jokes and topical songs with indecent *doubles entendres* would strive to amuse, while the dancers rested for a few brief minutes. Then back again—these puppets, these parasites of a civilized world, swaying, turning, gavotting to music which numbed the last remnants of their so-called brains.

The room itself was garishly ornamented, but most of the decoration was shadowed by the lighting, which, dim and multi-coloured, was considered seductive. The sofas around the walls held a miscellaneous collection of people.

A few were men of important positions and intelligence, but they were not the *habitués;* tonight, for them, was only a peep-show, a mere momentary relaxation from sterner realities.

Women—they had made the place a success, and they would keep it so, continuing to patronize it night after night, until another converted cellar would be discovered elsewhere. Beautiful, well-bred, fashionable women, with position, money, and children, craving excitement as a drunkard craves for drink.

Their calm indifference and air of boredom only a pose, seething with hungry desires for more—"give us thrills!"—"galvanize us to life!"—"shock us if you can!"—never satisfied, never replete with this dish of indecency, perverted sex, and dirt.

A young girl is entering, a debutante; maybe her mother has grown tired of chaperonage; or perhaps, this evening, she has escaped from that vigilant eye.

Breath-takingly lovely, as only youth can be when it is fresh and unspoiled, she looks around, her eyes wide and surprised, a little apprehensive—she is uncertain if she likes it or not.

The dancers, the insidiousness of the crude music, low lights, and warm moving bodies, are having their effect. She laughs, her mind is made up—what fun! . . . she must come again.

Another convert! In a year she will be an *habitué*, like the others, drugged with cheap sensations.

Rosemary and Ronald were in a secluded corner of the room, the mirrors around them reflecting and re-reflecting their profiles into a successive eternity. Ronald was the type of young man who is at his best in a restaurant.

He could not talk without a table in front of him and a band as an accompaniment. It is a complex which is only one of the many which have sprung up since home life became only for children and the bedridden.

A pretty woman, music, and drink were Ronald's idea of bliss. He thought himself in love with Diana; but had she not been the most beautiful woman he knew, and also the most socially chic, it is doubtful if he would have contemplated matrimony.

"Well, anyway," he said now, looking at Ian as he came in with Diana, and grinning in spite of his chagrin, "Diana is educating the fellow. When he first

51

appeared, I don't believe he knew what a cocktail was."

Rosemary laughed.

"I don't expect there's much that Diana hasn't taught him," she replied, somewhat maliciously, enjoying as the result of her words the angry expression on Ronald's face.

Since her opulent days had come to stay, Rosemary had become rather like a well-fed cat. She stretched her claws and sharpened them on the person nearest to her at the moment.

But she was too luxurious and too comfortable to worry one way or another, or to have any real emotions. She merely kept one ever-watchful eye on Lord Leadhold, and let other men come or go as they pleased.

Across the room Diana greeted Rosemary and Ronald with a wave of her hand, but did not come over to speak to them, as she would have done two months before. Then she and Ian became interested in their own conversation.

"Do you think she is falling in love with the man?" Ronald asked Rosemary.

"Perhaps—how should I know?" she replied. "I should think it most unlikely. Diana always preferred a more theatrical type—like you, Ronald dear."

"Why can't he go back to his place in Scotland, and stay there?" Ronald grumbled.

"Why don't you ask him?" Rosemary answered.

"I've a b—— good mind to." He spoke vehemently.

Rosemary glanced at him, slightly apprehensive. Ronald had had a good deal to drink, and when he was like that he was often carried away into doing mad things. Looking at him, Rosemary felt that if it ever came to a fight, Ronald would stand little chance against Ian.

"Don't be silly," she said sharply; "he will only be rude to you, and Diana will be furious."

"All the same," Ronald answered, subsiding a little, "it is damn' nonsense. I never see Diana these days."

"Do any of us?" said Rosemary. "However, give it time, and she is sure to come back."

"I only hope to God she does," Ronald said; "but unless someone drowns that damn' fellow, I don't see how we are going to get her back. . . . For goodness' sake let's go!"

He beckoned a waiter and asked for the bill.

At that very moment, as it happened, Diana was talking about them. After two months she had progressed very little further with Ian, and yet she in no wise intended to abandon the chase.

She had never forgotten for a moment her objective, and though, had she been frank with herself, she would have admitted that the pursuit was entertaining her, nevertheless she was not weakening.

Ian had taken her out night after night, day after day. They had dined together, they had raced, they had motored and flown, yet never was she quite certain that he was any nearer to falling in love with her than he had been on the first night they had dined together.

It was nearing the end of the season, and Diana decided that things must shortly come to a head. In a week or so, at the dictates of fashion, they would all be leaving London. Ian, she knew, was going to his castle in Scotland; she herself had various invitations, though she had not, as yet, made up her mind which to accept.

Already her friend, and, what was more important, her mother's friends, were beginning to talk about her. They had long since given up anticipating Diana's marriage, but they could not help speculating on this new affair. Diana found her part of being incessantly nice about and to someone she hated, beginning to wear upon her, and become wearisome.

She decided that she must, within a week, bring things to a climax. Ian must declare himself, and she would be able to turn him down, at the same time scorning him for desiring a love he had sneered at.

It was a harder task than she had anticipated, but she had no doubts of ultimately getting her own way. She was beautiful, she told herself, as she caught a glimpse of her reflection in a mirror opposite.

Then she saw Ronald on the same surface, and had an idea—a little jealousy might be good for Ian. She had often mentioned Ronald in the course of conversation, and now she pointed him out.

"He is a perfect darling," she said, "and I am very, very fond of him."

Ian contemplated the rather sulky-looking young man lounging beside Rosemary Makines.

"Don't you think he is divine to look at?" Diana continued.

"Very," Ian answered dryly.

In his opinion, Ronald looked as though he wanted a year's hard work and a good kicking.

Diana, disappointed by his answer, decided on another course.

"Let's go and talk to them," she said, rising to her feet. "I haven't seen Ronald for weeks."

She ran across the room, and Ian had no choice but to follow.

"Darling," she said to Rosemary, "we've come to talk to you. Ian is finding me so infinitely boring that I feel he will enjoy your company more than mine."

She separated Rosemary and Ronald, leaving Ian a place next to Rosemary.

Diana then drew a very willing Ronald into an intimate, half-whispered conversation. Ronald was far too surprised and pleased at this unexpected turn of events to be annoyed with Diana for her past neglect.

He immediately became animated and strove to amuse her. The bill he had asked for was sent away, and more champagne ordered, which, as it was after hours, eventually arrived in jugs.

"Come and dance," he begged Diana, knowing that he was in his element on the floor, for he was a perfect dancer, and was an expert at murmuring sweet nothings into the ears of his partners.

Diana acquiesced, and they rose and were soon moving rhythmically together, obviously enjoying themselves; but if Ian thought they were needlessly affectionate he gave no sign, and continued to talk gravely and politely to Rosemary. Only when they returned to the table did he assert himself.

"I hope you will forgive me if we go now—unless you care to stay alone?" he said. "But I have to be up early tomorrow morning, and I don't want to be too late."

"Up early—why?" Diana asked.

"I have to go away for a day or two," Ian answered.

Relieved, but slightly vexed that he had not told her before, Diana rose, knowing that it was no use arguing with him. She had already learned that Ian always went home when he pleased.

"Good night, darling," she said to Rosemary. "I shall see you tomorrow, Ronald."

Annoyed at being taken away so early, yet not wishing to be left behind, she got into the taxi outside.

"You are not angry with me for dancing with Ronald?" she asked.

"Why should I be?" Ian said, without a trace of deeper emotion in his voice.

"I wonder if I shall marry him," Diana went on.

"You are the only person who can decide that," Ian answered.

Yet, in spite of himself, he felt suddenly afraid.

He had not meant to fall in love with Diana. After their first meeting he had told himself she was shallow and worthless; but as he saw more and more of her, he realized that underneath that painted exterior there was real character hidden, and a charm which no man had yet discovered.

Exploration had always thrilled him; the determination he had expended on uncharted country, he now applied to seeking the heart he sensed beneath the barrier of unconcerned vanity.

Gradually, as the days passed, he fell in love with Diana, until he knew his affections to be hopelessly and irretrievably hers. Yet he swore he would make no sign, until he knew if she cared at all.

He was not going to make a fool of himself, to be carried away as the others had been; and though Diana appeared delighted to see him and obviously enjoyed his company, he did not believe she had as yet any depth of real regard for him.

Tonight, in spite of his apparent indifference, had tried his patience rather far. He had disliked Ronald, and he could not help being jealous of any man in whom Diana was interested. He knew she was spoilt, and he could not yet forgive her for Jack. But he believed that, once away from her shallow world, she would find herself.

His was not the blind, impetuous passion of a boy who knows nothing of human nature, but the deep love of a man of experience—the mature love which does not expect perfection, but seeks it even in the loved one's faults.

And thus, after consideration, and with his eyes fully open, Ian intended eventually to make Diana his wife.

He wanted her—her beauty thrilled him—her grace, her smile, her sweetness, made him adore her with the reverence of true love; her helplessness, her inability to do things for herself, her lack of strength, made him very tender; the touch of her soft hand, the magnetism of her beautiful body, her white neck, and her throat, made him throb with the passion of a lover.

But at the same time he was not oblivious to her failings; he hated her sudden bursts of uncontrollable temper, he hated the trivialities which amused her.

In the taxi he sat silent until they reached Grosvenor

Square. Then, as they stopped, Diana turned towards him.

The light of the street lamps shone on her hair and on a white shoulder from which her ermine cape had slipped. One of her hands fell lightly on his, and there was a faint fragrance about her, a strange, disturbing scent.

"If you are going away tomorrow," she said gently, "don't you think you had better say good-bye?"

She lifted her face to his, and no man could have misunderstood her invitation. But without a word, Ian merely opened the taxi door, and handed her out. He took her latchkey from her, and went up the steps.

Diana followed him, sheer fury rendering her silent. Then, as the heavy front door swung open, as she stepped past him into the darkness of the empty hall, he followed her in, and before she could turn round, before she could say a word, he had enfolded her in his arms.

His mouth found hers, and he kissed her, not roughly but with a passionate intensity which she had never known before.

Then he released her, and before she could recover her breath the front door slammed behind him, and he was gone.

Chapter 7

To Ian, that kiss meant a tremendous amount. To Diana, after her first momentary surprise, it was merely another triumphant step forward.

She went up to bed with her cheeks a little flushed

from his strength, but in a few moments she had forgotten him in a dreamless, peaceful sleep.

Nearly the whole night, in fact, until dawn was breaking, Ian walked about. He went through the deserted streets meeting only, here or there, a policeman or perhaps a street-walker who had been unfortunate.

He realized now how terribly he loved Diana. His nature had been pent up for so many years. He had repressed and subdued his feelings with all the sternness of Scottish reserve; but, like a volcano, they had erupted into an overwhelming passion and with a force he could not control.

He wanted Diana, and he meant to have her. For years he had achieved what others deemed impossible, simply through determination and will-power.

He had nourished those forces by winning whatever battle he attempted, and now the whole accumulation of this power was directed towards something he wanted more than he had ever wanted anything before.

As dawn broke, he went back to his hotel, and when he awoke from a short sleep the sunlight was shining in through his uncurtained window.

With his breakfast he found many letters, most of them invitations, for his father's friends were anxious to make his acquaintance. One from Scotland, from his keeper, assured him that the grouse would be good for the twelfth.

Over another he frowned. It was from Mrs. Melbourne, who had just returned from America and wanted to see him, to hear his story of Jack's death.

He was not pleased this morning at a reference to Jack. He wanted to forget the part that Diana had played. Jack, if he had never known her, would have lived a common enough Englishman's life; he would have hunted, fished, eventually married and settled down to a quiet, domestic existence in the country.

Ian thought of him now, thought of that lonely grave

in the jungle; with, as they had dug it, the carrion crows fluttering above.

Whatever happened, he could never forget those happy months they had spent together, and he would always remember that young, boyish face twisted in its agony of farewell.

His duty was clear. He had to see Mrs. Melbourne, and the sooner the better. With his usual courtesy, he cancelled the arrangements he had made for leaving London, and telephoned her house to say that he would be with her at noon.

Yet, try as he would, he could not forget for a moment, even with the memory of Jack refreshed in his mind, that kiss of the night before.

It still burned on his lips, and he could still feel that slight figure crushed in his arms, her startled ejaculation as he seized her, and the wide mystery of her eyes staring at him, her head thrown back, silhouetted against the glass door. Still he seemed to smell the scent of her hair and to feel the softness of her cheek against his.

Yet it was soberly enough that he travelled to Belgrave Square and was ushered into Mrs. Melbourne's presence.

She was a small, fragile woman with grey hair and nervous, restless movements. She gave him a thin hand to shake, and then in a gentle voice asked him to be seated.

It made his task doubly hard, when he saw immediately how much Jack must have meant to her. The whole room was redolent of him. A huge oil-painting was hung over the mantelpiece; Jack in khaki smiled down at Ian, and, so vivid was his presence, it almost seemed as though he stood in the room.

Everywhere there were photographs of him, as a baby, as a schoolboy, with his rowing eight, and, later, in his uniform. Mrs. Melbourne wore black, and it was obvious that she still mourned the son she would never see again.

Ian started the story of Jack's arrival in Africa. He told it swiftly until it came to the tragic circumstances of his death.

Though he had intended to tell Mrs. Melbourne everything, he found he could not mention Diana. He did not bring her name into it at all, though he blamed himself for a coward for omitting Jack's last words.

When he had finished speaking, Mrs. Melbourne wiped the tears from her eyes. It was a moment before she could control her voice, then she asked:

"And did he never tell you about his love for Diana Stanlier?"

Ian hesitated.

"Yes," he said at last, "he did mention her."

Mrs. Melbourne rose to her feet.

"She sent him to his death," she said.

"I think you misjudge her," Ian said quietly. "She could not marry Jack if she did not care for him. I think even Jack himself understood that."

"She is the type of woman no decent mother would care to see her son in love with," said Mrs. Melbourne. "She led him on, she encouraged him, she flirted with him. Oh, Mr. Carstairs, you do not know the nights I have listened to Jack pacing up and down his room, cursed with a love which would not let him sleep! A mother knows—and I knew, how miserable she was making him."

Ian said nothing, and Mrs. Melbourne after a moment continued:

"I prayed that he would get over it. When at last he talked of leaving me to go to Africa, I understood, and thought it was the best way. I hoped that in a few years he would return, cured of the disease that was posioning his life. He was all I had. My husband died many years ago, and Jack and I were inseparable companions. I think I may say quite truthfully he was devoted to me, until he met Diana Stanlier.

After that things were never the same. He was moody—a thing Jack had never been before. He was restless, and what was more—what broke my heart—he was unhappy. If she had not cared for him—no one could blame her for that—she could have sent him away at once. But she did not. She made use of him, and then, only when she was tired, threw him away, like an unwanted glove."

Ian had nothing to say. How could he? There was silence for many minutes. Then Mrs. Melbourne spoke again, as gently as she had at first.

"Forgive me," she said, "but you see I adored my son."

"I understand," Ian said. "I know how terribly you must feel this. I, too, loved Jack, and when his death gave me my life, I vowed I would do anything I could for him, or for anyone he loved."

"You mean you would do something for Diana Stanlier?" Mrs. Melbourne asked incredulously.

"Certainly." Ian spoke warmly. "Do not let us forget, Mrs. Melbourne, that Jack loved her. She could not be entirely unworthy to inspire the love of someone like Jack. Jack was a fine, courageous person, as you know. He had been brought up by you to know right from wrong, truth from insincerity. There is truth in Diana, and he knew it. Let us hope that she herself will know that truth before it is too late."

"Before she has sent many other men to their death, you mean," Mrs. Melbourne said bitterly.

Ian did not answer.

He spent more than an hour with Mrs. Melbourne. She told him much of Jack, all the tender things which a mother remembers and stores like treasures in her heart.

She showed numberless photographs of him, which

61

would have been very dull to anyone less sympathetic than Ian. But he understood how much she had longed to pour out her trouble to someone who had also loved Jack.

Jack had written to his mother so often of Ian. He had admired him, and knew him to be one of the finest men he had ever met. Ian saw some of these letters now, and he could not but be touched to see how wholeheartedly the young man had hero-worshipped him. He also felt a little humble; for what could he say now in gratitude for such affection?

And because of this he could not bear to leave Mrs. Melbourne tortured by the thought of her son lying in that lonely grave, and of Diana enjoying life day after day in the vortex of unthinking, uncaring gaiety.

And he strove, not only because he was fond of Diana but because he wished Mrs. Melbourne to find peace of mind, and the happiness of charitable thought, to arouse fairer feelings than that hatred which, while he understood it, seemed to him very pitiful.

But it was without avail, and when at last he left the house he was afraid that he himself was slightly antagonistic to its lonely and suffering occupant.

The whole interview left him with a furthered determination to rescue Diana from herself, not only because he loved her, and because he believed that he himself would find happiness with her, but because he knew she was worth saving while most of her contemporaries were not.

He was not unaware of the Stanlier history. No one who was interested in the story of England could be, and he was enough of a psycho-analyst to realize that Diana had interited much of the quality which had given her forebears names to be honoured.

He went down to Hellingly in Sussex that night, to stay with a man who was assisting him to buy bloodstock for Ronsa. Ian understood animals, and they understood him, and part of his belief in Diana was based on the fact that she, too, had a great love for horses and dogs.

She was a splendid rider. Ian had often ridden with her in the Row in the early morning, and once they had gone down to a friend at Newmarket, when she had helped exercise the stables, taking out on the gallops horses she had never seen before, with the courage and assurance of a born rider.

The only time Ian had ever seen her show any uncontrolled emotion was at the death of her dog.

They had been driving together in the country in his racing car, and as they returned home, with Diana at the wheel, they had seen a crowd outside her house in Grosvenor Square.

"An accident," Diana said. "We have one every hour opposite our house . . . just because I dislike them so much."

As they drew nearer, they saw that a taxi, drawn up beside the pavement, was obviously the cause of the trouble.

"Stop here," Ian said, "and I will go and see if anyone is hurt."

Diana put the brake on and drew the car to a standstill. She could not bear accidents of any sort, and the sight of blood made her feel physically sick.

Ian pushed his way to the front of the crowd; then, to his horror, he saw what had happened: Diana's dog, Swona, was lying in the gutter. He was still breathing faintly, but was obviously beyond help.

" 'E ran right across my wheel," the taxi-man was saying, over and over again, to anyone who would listen.

Ian attempted to lift the dog, but Diana, left alone in the car, had sensed what was wrong, and a moment later she was beside him, kneeling in the road with Swona's head in her lap.

63

She was very white, but she did not cry, only a little moan escaped her as the dog opened its eyes when it felt the familiar hand.

Seeing his mistress, he made a feeble, pitiable effort to wag his tail, then, as Diana patted him, speaking dog-language, he had a little convulsion, and fell back dead.

Ian had lifted the dog in his arms and taken a dazed Diana into the house, and later had arranged for the burial of the small body.

Only when she was alone with Ellen did Diana cry, and Ian, coming up to tell her what he had done, found her with her face buried in the old lady's shoulder, sobbing her heart out.

It was at Hellingly that he first saw the grey horse which was later to play a memorable part with Diana and himself. He had not meant to buy anything but brood-mares, but when he saw Starlight he could not resist him.

The beautiful grey had direct Arab blood in his veins, and the moment Ian saw him gallop he was filled with an immediate desire to possess him.

Although it seemed weakness to excuse his extravagance thus—he imagined Diana on Starlight . . . how lovely she would look astride the great horse; and he pictured her riding beside him over the moors in Ronsa.

The temptation was irresistible; he fell to it, in spite of the huge price required. He arranged for the horses to be dispatched to Ronsa, and returned to London the following day.

He was longing to see Diana, longing to hear her voice, to see her lovely face raised to his; and that one swift embrace had made him hungry for more.

He telephoned to her when he arrived, and thrilled as her voice answered, the gaiety and fresh vitality of her coming to him even through the dull medium of a telephone.

"Dine with you?" said Diana. "I'd adore it! Have you enjoyed your meanderings in the country?"

"I missed you," Ian answered, almost without meaning to—an unusually demonstrative remark for him.

He heard Diana give a little laugh.

"I am glad," she said. "I thought perhaps, to you, I was just like water off a duck's back. Have you really thought about me?"

"I will tell you tonight," Ian said, and rang off.

"I've got him!" Diana said, and she felt excitement rush over her in a little wave.

She was curiously elated, a little breathless, and at the same time impatient for the hours to pass. She dressed with unusual care, yet, when at last she was ready, she broke her usual custom and did not go upstairs to Ellen.

She suddenly felt she could not bear to hear her old nurse praising Ian. She hated him, she told herself. She did not want his praises to be ringing in her ears as she went down to meet him. Tonight revenge was to be really sweet.

Her maid was packing, for tomorrow—though she had not yet told Ian—she was leaving for the South of France. She was going to pay a number of visits, and her maid was to forward her heavy luggage while she herself left in an airplane at noon.

Diana had her own private airplane; she could pilot it herself, but when she went on long journeys her parents insisted that she took a mechanic with her.

It was an open two-seater Moth, painted silver-grey, with a line of deep blue. She was going to stay a night or so in Paris, and a suitcase contained her clothes. Her maid was used to these journeys, and had devised a way of packing an immense amount into a very small space.

When at last she went downstairs, she stood for a moment outside the library door. Her heart was thumping a little, and she felt a thrill of anticipation. She had him, she told herself.

Then she entered the room, with a sweet smile on her lips.

Chapter 8

THEY dined very quietly that night at a grill-room.

Over dinner, Ian talked of ordinary things—of the horses he had just bought, and of his plans for Scotland. When there was a pause in the conversation, Diana said:

"I am going away tomorrow—to Paris, and then on to the South of France. My first visit is to Violet Longden." Ian seemed interested, and she continued: "I expect Ronald will be there, he nearly always is."

Ian did not rise to her bait.

"That will be amusing," was all he said.

She was looking very beautiful tonight, but she was a little tired. She had spent a strenuous season enjoying herself; there were shadows under her eyes, and she was paler than when he had first met her. It became her, that rather fragile air, but Ian thought she spoilt herself by the artificial darkness of her eyelashes, and the violent crimson of her mouth.

Diana had naturally a wonderful complexion, and there was really no need for her to use the same amount of cosmetic as other women, but fashion made her follow, sheep-like, the dictation of the experts—whoever they may be—who ordained what women shall look like.

A sudden thought of Jean Ross made Ian contrast the two. He wondered how Jean would look painted and decorated like Diana, and dressed in expensive clothes. Ian hated all artificiality, but especially for a woman to be very much "made-up".

It had partly originated from an incident which had happened to him in Egypt. He had been staying at Luxor on a journey to the desert, and with him had been a young man who had just come out from England.

Tony Tyson was a nice boy, and he was spending a short holiday with Ian before he returned to Manchester, where his father had a huge factory.

He was very young, and had met very few people, and Ian had promised his father he would look after him on this particular holiday. Mr. Tyson had done him a good turn on several occasions, and Ian was glad to have a chance of returning the compliment.

After they had spent a day or two seeing the tombs and temples, they found it more amusing to play tennis in the gardens of the Winter Palace or to drift lazily up and down the Nile in the electric canoes.

Tony was thrilled with the world-famous snake-charmer who took them to the deserted gardens of the Grand Hotel, which had been burnt to the ground many years previously, and there charmed from their holes two cobras and a scorpion.

There was no doubt of his genuineness, but to prove it beyond any chance of contradiction, they took the old man in a car, far out into the desert, and there, miles from his home, bade him use his powers. He found four snakes immediately, and carried them back to Luxor in triumph.

Unfortunately, Ian was recalled to Cairo for twenty-four hours on important business, and when he returned he found that Tony had made the acquaintance of a woman who was staying in the hotel.

She was an attractive brunette of uncertain age—the sort of woman who has spent most of her life in the East and who wanders about from hotel to hotel with apparently little object in view except to pick up new acquaintances.

Her dark hair was parted, Madonna-like, in the middle. She had long, sweeping, eyelashes, blackened, of course, and the slight anaemic sallowness of her cheeks was hidden by a vivid but well-put-on rouge.

Her over-painted mouth was grotesque to Ian, but was obviously inviting to the very young.

Olive Phillips wore strange, exotic clothes, but their bizarre colourings and soft folds suited her. All too soon it was evident to Ian that Tony was infatuated.

He was sorry, for Tony was a healthy, clean boy, and Ian had taken an instinctive dislike to Mrs. Phillips. She must be old enough to be his mother, he thought angrily, but he could not be sure.

As the days went by, Ian saw increasingly little of Tony. Every morning he made some excuse or other for disappearing up the Nile with his new friend, and he was obviously becoming more and more enamoured of her.

At last Ian spoke to him. He had heard several none-too-savoury tales about the lady in question, not that he believed scandal, but the sources of his information were this time infallible.

"You are making a fool of yourself, young man," he said, as gently as possible, one night.

"It is my own life—I shall do as I please," Tony answered. "If you think I am going back to Manchester, to that —— factory, at the end of the week, you are mistaken. I am going away with Olive—we will travel together to Assouan, and there I am going to make her happy. She has had a hard life," he added.

Ian laughed, a hard, mirthless laugh.

"They always have," he said dryly.

"I know you don't like her, and if you think I am being a fool, I don't care," Tony said hotly. "I love

Olive, and she loves me, and that's surely enough for any man."

Seeing how serious the boy was, Ian became grave.

"What about your father?" he said, thinking of the old man who adored this only son of his, and who looked to him to take over the factory and its responsibilities in the near future.

Tony hesitated only for a moment.

"I am going with Olive," he said. "Her husband will divorce her, she assures me, and then we can be married."

"I don't know how you are going to keep her if your father cuts you off," Ian said.

"He won't. Even if he does, it will make no difference to Olive."

Ian rather doubted that, but he had no proof, and seeing there was no more to be said he went to bed, but not to sleep. He did some hard thinking before the dawn brought another day. All night he turned over in his mind the name "Phillips".

He seemed to have a vague memory that he had known someone of that name, and then he suddenly remembered.

Two days later they were all three sitting at dinner. The dining-room of the Winter Palace looks across the Nile to the hills beyond where, in the Valley of the Kings, the tombs are being excavated.

Outside was one of those still, purple nights which one only finds in the East, but no one paid any heed, for inside there were lights and laughter.

It was a gala night, and people had come in from all the other hotels. The band was playing the same tunes which were being played all over the world—hot American syncopation—and one of the band in nasal tones sang the stupid accompanying words.

Mrs. Phillips, dressed in a clinging gown of peacock-blue brocade, with huge emeralds in her ears, and rings to match on her hands—greedy hands, Ian thought

69

them, with sharp, pointed nails—was holding young Tony entranced.

Ian sat back, surveying the scene dispassionately. He smiled at the futility of the Americans, who, dancing to tunes created in their own home towns, imagined they were seeing Eastern life.

The same food was being served to them as was being served in London, in Paris, in Berlin, in New York; the people dancing around all believed they were getting full value for the money they had spent in travelling.

They went from Hotel Ritz to Hotel Ritz, finding the same atmosphere, the same people, even the same waiters.

Tonight the prices were automatically raised; a gala evening meant little else, except that the management, in magnificent generosity, gave away a few paper hats and several paper streamers, totalling perhaps an expense of sixpence per guest, while the bill for dinner was trebled.

However, there was no dissatisfaction. Women who were Tartars for propriety at home wore jockey caps, and threw streamers at complete strangers. Men who were respected as dignified city magnates blew tin whistles, a sun-bonnet or dunce's cap concealing their grey hairs.

And, while the gala continued, Ian, watching Tony, felt sad to think how much he had to learn before he could distinguish the gold from the dross.

While there was a pause in the dancing, a thin, nervous-looking man, in somewhat soiled white ducks, appeared in the doorway. He had evidently been travelling, and seemed tired and rather dusty.

He glanced at the gay throng who, beyond an impertinent stare or two, took no notice of him. And then his eyes alighted on Ian. He walked across to him and held out his hand.

"Hullo, Carstairs," he said; "I am glad to see you. But I have had a hell of a journey to get here."

Then he saw Olive.

"Why, Mother!" he said. "What a surprise!"

Olive Phillips' face would have been as white as the table-cloth had her make-up permitted it. As it was, her animation gone and with an angry expression, she looked in a moment twenty years older.

"What are you doing here?" she asked harshly.

But before he could answer, Tony, with the gaucherie of youth, had ejaculated, "Your son!" and risen to his feet.

Ian gave one look at the infuriated woman, then introduced the two men.

"This is Jim Phillips," he said to Tony, "who has been working up-country for the last eight years. It has been a tough time, hasn't it, Jim? But then, we beggars can't be choosers."

Tony did not miss the glance Ian gave to Olive Phillips' jewels, and to her expensive dress.

It was only chance that had made Ian remember a desolate station where he stayed for a week some years ago; only chance that an attack of malaria to his host had let him learn that Jim Phillips always sent his money home, and that the cheques were made payable to "Mrs. Phillips".

It was a common enough name, but there was a vague resemblance between mother and son, and once he had connected the two there was no doubt in his mind that he was right in his supposition.

Rather a chastened Tony journeyed home to Manchester and work a week later, and Ian had hated an over-painted woman ever since.

What was afterwards a comedy might so easily have been the tragedy of a foolish young man, and if Ian had made a female enemy, he knew he had in Manchester a staunch friend for life.

As Diana made up her lips from a tiny enamelled vanity-box studded with diamonds, Ian thought how far lovelier she would look without her make-up, but he wisely said nothing, knowing that words have never convinced any woman.

Their dinner had been almost a silent meal, there was a tension between them, an atmosphere unnatural as the calm before a storm. They left; Ian's car was outside.

It was only eleven o'clock, and Diana was surprised when he drove her home, but she said nothing, and as they reached her front door, he asked:

"May I come in for a moment? I want to talk to you."

"Do," she said, and led the way to her own sitting-room.

It was quite a small room, but exquisitely furnished in the pretty colours which Diana loved—sea-green walls, with flaming hangings covering the windows and the deep, soft sofas. She turned on only a light or two, setting an exquisitely dim and romantic stage for herself.

The window on to the balcony was open, and the curtains swung in the slight night breeze, while the distant hum of traffic came to their ears like very gentle music.

She offered Ian a cigarette, but he refused it, standing a little stiffly in front of the fireplace, as if he were rather nervous. Diana sank down on to a sofa, the bright brocade making a perfect setting for her in her simple white dress. Like a demure child, she folded her hands in her lap, and waited.

Then at last, Ian spoke what was in his heart.

"Diana," he said, "I love you. The first time I came to this house, I was prepared to love you, you had already charmed me, already drawn me to you, though we had not met. And then for a moment I was so struck by your callousness and lack of feeling, that I think, for a little while, I hated you. But now I know you have a heart, and I want it. I love you, Diana—

72

you are beautiful, but you are more than that. I want you to love me—and I want you to marry me."

He spoke very quietly, but there was a depth of feeling in his voice which no woman had ever heard before.

Diana sat quite still with her eyes cast down, the shadow of a smile on her lips. Ian stepped forward and dropped on one knee beside her, putting his arms around her yielding body.

"Answer me, darling," he said hoarsely, "answer me!"

Just for one single moment she rested in his embrace. Then she sprang to her feet and faced him, her eyes flashing, colour in her cheeks, her whole body pulsatingly alive.

"That is where I wanted you!" she cried. "That is where I've tried and schemed to get you, where you should be—on your knees!"

At her words Ian stiffened, and then very slowly rose to his feet.

"What do you mean?" he asked, his voice very quiet and low.

"You despised me—you insulted me—the first day you came here," Diana answered. "You spoke of 'my sort of love', and I swore then that you should ask for that love—that you should want it . . . and behold!—I have succeeded!"

She laughed a little wildly.

"Down on your knees you have asked for it, for the love that you sneered at. . . . Now it is my turn. I hate you—I loathe you! . . . You can go now, and I never want to see you again!"

Ian still stood gazing at her. Few people had ever seen him lose his temper, but underneath a rigid control he had the strong, wild temper of the Highlander. Really aroused, he was ruthless in his anger.

He seldom took offence, and it was difficult indeed to urge him beyond a certain stern gravity, if people or things annoyed him. But on occasion the blood he had inherited from generation upon generation of fierce-fighting chieftains would make him formidable indeed to one who had offended.

Diana now half sensed what she had done, for in his eyes blazed the fury of a man who has been driven too far—a man who controls himself with difficulty.

For one apprehensive moment she waited, silent with a sudden fear—then he turned without saying a word, and walked swiftly from the room.

She was triumphant, she had attained her objective; yet she felt curiously unelated, and her only sensation was of being utterly weary.

Chapter 9

DIANA woke in the morning to the flurry and bustle which always occurs before one leaves on a long journey.

Lord and Lady Stanlier were also departing that day for New York. They were going on a visit to Lady Stanlier's sister, who had married an American, and whom they had not seen for several years.

They said a fond farewell to their daughter, and left several needless instructions for her well-being. Immediately they had gone, Diana collected her hand baggage and prepared to depart also.

"I shall be back in about a month, Janet," she said to her maid.

"And I hope you have a good time, m'lady."

Janet gave a last-minute tweak to Diana's coat,

brushed off an invisible speck of dust, and saw her safely into the car which was to take her to Hanworth Aerodrome.

Just as they were about to start, the butler hurried down the steps with a message.

"What is it?" Diana asked.

"You are wanted on the telephone, m'lady—it is Hanworth Aerodrome speaking."

Wondering if something were wrong, Diana returned to the house.

"Hullo!" she said down the telephone.

"Is that Lady Diana Stanlier?" asked a voice.

"Yes," Diana answered; "do you want me?"

"I am speaking for your pilot," came the answer. "Fog is reported over the Channel, and he is anxious to start as soon as possible. He will have the 'plane ready for you the moment you arrive, if you will proceed at once to the usual ground."

"Thank you—I quite understand," Diana answered. "Tell Stephens I will be there as soon as possible."

"Thank you, my lady."

With a click the speaker rang off.

The morning was not sunny, but quite fine, and it was surprising that there should be a fog at that time of year. However, English weather is notoriously unreliable, and Diana gave instructions to the chauffeur to drive quickly.

As they hurried along through Hammersmith and on to the Great West Road, Diana, for the first time that morning, thought of the night before.

She smiled a little at the memory of Ian's repressed fury. There was no doubt that she had aroused his anger, and just for a moment, she confessed to herself, she had been frightened that she had gone too far.

She was not quite certain from what cause her fear had sprung—after all, he could not hurt her physically. Yet, somehow, that great man, with his clenched hands,

75

staring at her, had made her heart beat quicker than usual, and she knew that she had instinctively stepped back, as though to avoid him.

In a way, she was sorry to think that she would not see Ian again. He had interested her, apart from the zest which the subtle drama of her intentions had added to what, ordinarily, would have been quite an amusing companionship.

How little she really knew him! He had evaded her usual quick diagnosis, and remained in many respects a closed book. She thought of how furious he would be with her today, and quite suddenly she laughed out loud, and afterwards dismissed him from her mind.

She arrived at Hanworth—that charming club, which is a converted country house. The garden was bright with flowers; porters greeted her, and seized her luggage from the car.

Remembering her instructions, she hurried quickly through the garden to the field of embarkation.

There she saw her airplane waiting, the pilot already in his seat. As she hurried towards it, an instructor came forward with her helmet and goggles, which she always left in the 'plane.

She put them on, and as she was doing so her luggage was speedily stored away.

"You had better hurry, Lady Diana," said the instructor, smiling at the care with which she adjusted her helmet. "Your pilot is getting impatient."

"It looks a good enough day for flying," said Diana.

"One can never be sure," was the answer. "Anyway, he says he has had a telephone message from Le Bourget, reporting fog."

He assisted Diana to scramble into the front seat. The pilot, goggled, with his earphones attached, was bending down in his cockpit.

"Is anything wrong?" Diana asked.

His answer was lost in a roar as the two mechanics

swung the propeller and the engine started. However, as she looked back over her shoulder, he shook his head, and she was satisfied.

A moment later they lifted off the ground, flying higher and higher as they went. There were few clouds and a very light wind, and their passage was quite smooth. Diana connected her earphones, and adjusted herself comfortably, preparing to enjoy her trip.

She loved flying, and already had done many hours' solo, but she was lazy enough to appreciate that when another person was in control, she could contemplate the scenery and think without interruption.

They were moving at a good pace. Below, the land seemed to be getting farther and farther away. Diana was suddenly conscious that they were rising all the time, and that the air was beginning to get cooler.

"Why are we going so high?" she asked down the mouthpiece facing her.

"Fog," came the answer abruptly to her ears.

Soon the land grew fainter and fainter, and in a few moments they were flying above the clouds. They must be up about six thousand feet, Diana thought, and wrapped her coat more warmly around her, adjusting an extra scarf which she always kept handy on the shelf in front.

Diana had had a swift lunch before she left home—only a few sandwiches and some coffee—for they timed out at 12.30, and she was not very hungry.

She was disappointed that they were flying so high, she loved seeing the houses and land beneath her. She enjoyed the Channel, with its long expanse of green and deep blue.

It fascinated her to see the ships and to watch the jagged outline of the French coast getting nearer and nearer, until they roared over it, to see the long, straight French roads like white ribbons, journeying on and on, seemingly unbroken, until they reached the South.

Being at a great height always affected Diana a little,

and now she felt drowsy; her head nodded, and she slept. When she awoke she looked at her watch, and found it was three o'clock.

They should have landed at Le Bourget long before this, she thought, but they were still above the clouds, and it was intensely cold.

"The fog has delayed us terribly," she said.

"We are all right—don't worry," came the answer, and Diana was reassured.

She ate some chocolate, and powdered what portion of her nose she could find beneath the goggles. This delay was boring. She had promised herself a cocktail at the Ritz by six o'clock, and before that there were several friends she had wished to notify of her arrival.

She loved Paris, and never had a lonely moment in that gay city, for not only had she many acquaintances who lived there permanently but she was also sure to find unexpected friends among the crowd who always gathered in the Ritz bar for their evening cocktail.

When she looked at her watch again, it was four o'clock.

"I say—this is absurd," she said impatiently into the mouthpiece. "I shall be so late. Can't you go down lower and see where we are?"

"It is impossible, I am afraid," came the muffled answer. "Please don't worry—you are quite all right."

"But this is ludicrous," Diana protested. "Are you quite sure that you have got your bearings correctly?"

"Certainly," was the reply.

"We have been three and a half hours already," she said.

"And we are not there yet," came the answer.

Really, Diana thought, Stephens was a fool. She should have piloted the 'plane herself. He was a good mechanic, she reflected, but as it happened he had not often been her pilot. She began to get a little worried, as they still stayed high above the clouds.

On and on they went, still moving, Diana guessed, at about a hundred and thirty miles an hour. They must be miles beyond Paris, she thought some time later, unless they had come in a complete circle.

"Look here, Stephens," she said at last, "this is absurd. Take the machine down until I can see where we are."

"I am afraid it is impossible," was the reply.

"I will take the responsibility," Diana answered. "Kindly do as you are told."

She waited for him to obey, but to her anger there was no downward swerve. They flew straight on without varying their height.

"Stephens! Will you kindly do what you are told?" she said; the pilot said nothing.

What was she to do? she wondered. Stephens must have gone raving mad. She had no idea where they were, but she reflected that they must have travelled nearly five hundred miles since leaving Hanworth.

What was she to do? Apparently orders were useless.

"What is the matter, Stephens?" she asked gently, but still he did not answer.

Diana became desperate. She was also not a little frightened.

"Stephens, will you answer me? What is the matter?"

But still he did not reply, and now Diana was really panic-stricken. There was nothing more to say. She felt impotent, helpless, and terrified.

She clung to the sides of the 'plane, thinking at any moment they might crash, that Stephens must have fainted as he did not answer her; but the airplane went on and on, swiftly, easily, without altering its altitude.

She was too frightened to cry or even to do anything but sit tight-lipped, her face deathly pale, but after a while the tension lessened. Nothing happened—they just went on and on.

Diana's thoughts were chaotic. They ranged swiftly over everyone she knew, everything she cared for—

she thought of Ian . . . even he could not cope with a situation like this, she reflected, and laughed a little hysterically at her own idea. Physical force against a lunatic in the air would be useless.

If only she had a parachute! She remembered, shame-facedly, how often she had scoffed at the idea when her anxious parents had suggested it!

On and on they went—until suddenly, when it seemed like a nightmare that would never end, the machine dropped its nose. They were going down!

"Where are we?" Diana asked. There was no answer.

Down—down—through the clouds, which brushed soft and damp against her cheeks, down until a moment later she saw the earth beneath them, and stared, puzzled.

They were over a hilly country, with rivers, and far away, on the extreme east, she could see the sea. Down they went, lower and lower, until directly beneath them she could see a flat landing-ground; yet obviously not an official aerodrome.

"Thank God," she thought to herself, "I am safe after all!"

They turned, heeling over so swiftly that Diana felt dazed. The earth seemed to rush up to meet her, but the 'plane righted itself, and, instinctively, she could not help appreciating the pilot's professional handling. Then they were taxi-ing, bump, bump, across the ground, and at last came to a standstill.

"Stay where you are—don't move," came the order through the earphones. She turned in surprise. "We are only filling up."

"I am going to get out," Diana said, and pulled the 'phones out of the connecting-rod.

She undid the belt round her waist, and sprang up. As she did so, she saw two men hurrying across the ground with petrol-cans in their hands. Then, to her surprise, she felt strong hands on her shoulders, forcing her back into her seat.

"Leave me alone!" she said sharply, and as she spoke turned her head. Then utter astonishment made her do what she was told, for the pilot had raised his goggles, and facing her was Ian.

"What are you doing?" she asked angrily, but her voice sounded weak even to her own ears.

"I am filling up," Ian answered.

"Where are we going to? Why are you here? Where is Stephens?"

Diana fired all her questions at him rapidly, but he took no notice. Half standing in his seat, he still kept one hand on her shoulder, as he directed the distribution of the petrol.

"Don't be absurd, and let me out," Diana said, shaking his hand off, but Ian said sharply:

"It doesn't matter how much scene you make—these men will take no notice of you."

Then, before Diana could collect her whirling thoughts and decide on a direct action, Ian called out "Contact!" The propeller was swung, and with a roar they were off again.

Up they rose, but this time they flew below the clouds, and Diana, as her bewilderment faded away, began to take stock of her surroundings. It was obvious to her that they were still heading north. Mining districts were in sight, a small town or two, and then in the distance she saw the outskirts of Glasgow.

"Why is he doing this?" she asked herself, and readjusting the earphones asked Ian the same question. "Why are you doing this? Where are we going?" she cried.

To her fury, there was no reply. They passed over Loch Katrine, leaving Ben Lomond grim and austere on their left.

"He's mad!" she kept telling herself, yet reason told her that Ian was extraordinarily sane.

"We can't be going to Ronsa," she thought; "he would not dare take me there!"

Yet at that moment she knew him capable of anything.

On and on they went. She was growing hungry and cramped in her confined position. She would never forgive him for this—never! She would get even with him for this, Diana raged furiously. Yet her helplessness dawned upon her mind.

"Ian, please—what are we going to do?" she pleaded.

Still there was no answer, and she reproached herself for that momentary lack of pride. She even tried to swear, but the words on her lips seemed wasted and as useless as her anger.

Why had this man come into her life? Diana asked. Why had she been such a fool as to try to avenge herself?

Far better have let him go that first day, thinking what he liked, and she would have forgotten him as speedily as she had forgotten the object which had brought him to her.

On and on . . . would they never stop, the roar of the engine singing in her ears? She was tired, and yet at the same time her nerves were taut with the tension of the situation.

On and on . . . there was the sea now, on the left of them. There were no towns to be seen, only mountains, lochs, and occasionally a tiny hamlet nestling in the valley in the shadow of the cloud-covered peaks above it.

On and on . . . till, suddenly, they were dropping. It was getting dark; what sun there was had already sunk beneath the horizon. Then, as they dropped, Diana had her first glimpse of the island of Ronsa.

She was conscious first of the vast spaces of the Atlantic; it seemed to stretch until the sea and the sky were intermingled, so that there was no dividing-line. But its waves were breaking, white and irregular, against the shores of a tiny island, which grew larger as they flew towards it.

She saw the Castle, a dark grey square from the air, the vast expanse of moor behind, with a white croft or two like pebbles on its surface.

Down . . . down . . . till the green landing-ground was beneath them; and they dropped until, preluded with the usual first quick bump, they were taxi-ing across it.

At one end Diana perceived an airplane shed, its corrugated iron roof shining, as though it were newly erected. Almost opposite the shed Ian stopped, and two men ran out towards them.

What was she going to say to him? Diana wondered, ignoring for the moment the question which rang again and again in her mind—what was he going to do with her here?

She rose to her feet, her legs cramped and stiff from her long journey. A moment later Ian was assisting her to the ground. She pulled her helmet from her head, shaking her hair from her eyes, and facing him proudly, she said:

"Perhaps you will now explain what this means."

Chapter 10

IAN ignored her.

He turned aside and spoke in a strange language, which she recognized as Gaelic, to the men who were moving the machine into the shed.

"I am speaking to you," Diana said sharply.

"So I can hear," Ian answered. "We will go into the house first. This is hardly a suitable place for explanations."

With her chin raised, her head in the air, Diana walked beside him till they came to a gate, which led into the Castle grounds.

"There is rather a splendid view from here," Ian said, in a conversational tone, stopping for a moment and pointing towards the mainland, where mountains peaked high above grey cliffs against which the waves were breaking.

Diana said nothing. She merely waited until he chose to move on again.

"I am sorry you are not interested," Ian continued, still in a light and charming tone of voice, "because I am afraid you will have plenty of time to admire it in the course of the next few weeks."

Diana could not remain silent after that.

"Next few weeks!" she echoed. "What are you talking about? Are you mad?"

"Quite," Ian answered. "That is why, I expect, I desire your company."

"But I don't know what you are talking about," said Diana, bewildered. "Why you have brought me here, what you are doing, I don't know and I don't understand. I shall leave at once."

"This is an island," Ian said. "The mainland, which has a regular if sparse train-service, is over three miles away. Of course," he added reflectively, "if you feel capable of swimming that distance . . ."

Diana stamped her foot in a sudden fury.

"Will you tell me why you have brought me here?" she cried.

"All in due course," Ian answered quietly, and stood aside for her to enter the Castle.

Inside the door, an oldish woman with grey hair was awaiting them.

"My Housekeeper," Ian explained. "I am afraid she

84

only speaks Gaelic, but she will look after you to the best of her ability. Her name is Margaret."

He turned to the woman, and evidently gave her some instructions, for she beckoned Diana, who by this time was too bewildered to protest, up the wide oak staircase. She led the way to the huge State-Room of the Castle.

Had Diana been there in any other circumstances, she would have admired this room exceedingly. A big log fire, burning in the medieval stone fireplace, threw out a warm, golden light, striving to disperse the shadows caused by the great carved oak four-poster bed, with its tapestry hangings and embroidered coverlet.

Tapestry also framed the windows, which looked over the garden and the sea. A white bearskin rug lay in front of the fire, and its fellow was before the massive dressing-table.

But Diana had no eyes for the beauty of the room. She was contemplating—speechless, because no one could understand her—the sight of a maid unpacking her suitcase.

With obvious gestures, Margaret asked her which dress she would put on. Through an open door, Diana saw a bath steaming invitingly, and suddenly she felt it was hopeless for the moment to refuse to fall in with Ian's arrangements.

She could not leave the island tonight, unless he chose to send her, and he evidently would not discuss the matter with her until after dinner.

She was also conscious that she was extremely hungry—she had had no food for eight hours. She shrugged her shoulders, and started to undress.

In her bath, the warm water refreshing and easing her stiff limbs, she tried to review the situation sensibly, but still the explanation of such conduct escaped her.

Perhaps, she thought, he had brought her here as a

joke. For all she knew, there might be a large house-party awaiting her downstairs.

She was not very confident that her hope would prove correct, yet, glancing at her reflection in the mirror when she was finally dressed, she felt herself equal to cope with anyone—"Or no one," she added.

The boom of the gong, which echoed through the house, brought her slowly down the stairs. Ian was waiting for her in the hall, and as she descended she posed a little, as all women do when they know that their entrance is extremely effective.

Her long white tea-gown of web-like lace trailed in a pointed train behind her. The wide-sleeves were edged with fur, and she wore a bunch of crimson carnations at her waist.

Ian wore a kilt, and the velvet jacket of Highland evening dress. The Carstairs tartan was dark green, crimson, and white, and he looked magnificently in keeping with his surroundings.

Dinner was not served in the huge Dining-Room, but in a small intimate room leading from a comfortable library, which Diana had barely time to view as they passed through it.

The dinner was perfect, but Diana was so hungry that she would have enjoyed an even less succulent meal. She accepted a glass of champagne, which quickly revived her, so that she felt stronger to face the explanations which would come later.

They were waited on by kilted servants, who moved silently to and fro with massive silver dishes, which Diana rightly guessed were very old and valuable.

While the servants were still in the room, Ian talked easily on ordinary topics of conversation. They might have been sitting at the Embassy, with many friends around them, instead of being unconventionally alone in this strange, out-of-the-world spot.

At that moment, Diana was half amused at the whole situation—it was so incredible, and so utterly unlike anything she had met before in her life. She imagined how thrilled Rosemary would be at the whole story, and visualized her own mischievous amusement at Ronald's jealousy and fury.

But then, unquieteningly, came the question, how soon would she be able to tell them, and what other chapters would be added to her tale before she could?

A sudden wave of insecurity made her glance at Ian. Sitting at the opposite ends of the table, they might have been husband and wife, and at the thought Diana put down her glass, for her hand was unsteady.

"Have you finished?" Ian asked at length. "Shall we go into the other room?"

Diana rose, and passed through the door held open for her. The Library into which she walked was a long room with stone-mullioned windows, which in the daytime looked on to the garden, but which were now closed by heavy velvet hangings.

A big open fireplace held a log fire, and in front of it lay two dogs. The length of the room was cleverly shortened by a huge Chinese screen, creating an intimate and cosy space round the fire.

"Won't you sit down?" Ian asked, pointing to a large, comfortable sofa.

Diana shook her head.

"I think the time has now come for some explanation," she said, but at that moment the door opened and a servant entered with coffee.

Frustrated again, she sank petulantly on to the proffered sofa, accepting her coffee, and even a small liqueur, as pleasantly as she could. There was silence for a moment between them, and that silence seemed to be charged with so much tensity that Diana rushed hastily into speech.

"What a strange sword!" she said, pointing to where it hung above the mantelpiece, in an ornate gold sheath studded with jewels, amethysts, cornelians, and Scotch pearls.

"It belonged to my great-great-grandfather," Ian said. "It was hung there by his father. You see that table underneath it? On it is written, 'He that lives by the sword shall die by the sword.'"

"Did he?" Diana said, sipping her coffee.

"Yes," Ian answered. "His parents begged him not to enter the Army, but he insisted, even running away from home to do so. They never forgave him, and when he died, their only memorial was to hang the sword where you see it, with that tablet underneath."

"How hard-hearted," Diana said.

"Do you think so?" Ian replied. "Personally, I believe as my forebears did, that we should receive just treatment for our deeds. Wouldn't you treat a murderer as a murderer?"

Diana hesitated.

"Yes, I suppose so."

"And a woman who behaves as a harlot like a harlot?"

Diana put down her cup a little hastily, and rose to her feet. She sensed an underlying meaning from the tone of Ian's voice. She was suddenly desperately afraid.

"Why have you brought me here?" she asked.

"I thought it would interest you," Ian replied, lighting a cigarette, and watching her as he did so.

"I want to know the truth," she insisted.

"Perhaps, strange as it may seem, I desired your companionship."

"I wish to leave first thing tomorrow morning," Diana said. "I do not understand you, or your farcical behaviour, and, what is more, I don't wish to."

As he did not answer, she repeated,

"I shall leave tomorrow morning."

"I am afraid not."

"You fool!" she exclaimed. "Do you think you can keep me here, and that I can vanish without anyone making inquiries?"

"Your parents sailed for America only this morning," Ian answered, bending down casually to pat the head of the dog at his feet, "and I took the opportunity of wiring your friends in the South of France that your visit was unavoidably postponed."

"How dare you!" Diana cried.

"I have already answered that remark," was the reply.

"But why—why . . ." Diana's voice failed her for words, for anything with which to combat this hopeless situation.

She felt frustrated and impotent, standing there while he regarded her with negligent amusement, as if she were an angry child.

"I am going to bed," she said sharply, and turned abruptly towards the door.

"But of course!" Ian sprang to his feet.

She passed through the door he held for her with her head high, but he would not be ignored. He followed her into the great Hall, and there handed her a massive silver candlestick.

"I hope you will find everything you require," he said courteously. "Tomorrow I have many things to show you."

She moved towards the stairs, and walked away from him with the greatest dignity she could command, uneasily conscious that he watched her progress.

She went into her room. The firelight shone brightly on the hearth and ceiling, only the great four-poster was in shadow.

Diana did not light the thick candles on her dressing-table, or their counterparts, which stood like sentries beside the bed; instead she gazed contemplatively into the flames. She was a little unnerved by all that had happened that strange day—a little apprehensive of tomorrow.

Then a step outside startled her. Slowly the door swung open, and Ian entered.

"What do you want?" she asked . . . needlessly, for with an agonizing certainty she knew the answer.

He walked slowly towards her, but she stepped away from him.

"Leave my room!" she cried, but her voice quavered, and the words failed to sound commanding even to herself.

"You offered to kiss me last night," Ian said, his voice slow and quiet, but with an underlying tone of mockery which stung her.

He reached out his arm and clasped her wrist to draw her towards him, but with a swift movement she freed herself and sprang away from him. She ran to the other end of the room, and against the folds of the tapestry curtains stood palpitating.

Ian laughed.

"So shy," he said. "I would have believed otherwise."

"How dare you!" Diana breathed.

"*You* dared me," he answered. "Come!"

He held out his arms, seeming in his great height to dominate the room.

"No!" Diana defied him, her head thrown back, her hands clenched at her sides, but her breath came quickly and her breasts throbbed under their covering of thin lace.

"I want you, Diana"—and his voice was deep with desire.

Wildly Diana sought escape. She glanced feverishly round the room—but she was imprisoned. She was alone with Ian in this desolate Castle, save for servants to whom she could not make herself understood.

She was terrified, but the Stanlier pride kept her outwardly courageous.

"I despise and detest you," she said slowly and feelingly. "Does that attract you?"

"Immensely," he answered, smiling. "A complacent woman is often a bore."

He dropped his arms, but moved a step further towards her.

"This farce has gone far enough," Diana said fiercely. "Leave me, or . . ."

She hesitated.

"Or what?" prompted Ian. "What will you do?"

His arms enclosed her, she fought against him wildly, and there was a sound of rending.

Breathless, her hair dishevelled, her shoulder bare through the torn lace, she pushed him from her for a second. Very lovely she was at that moment, her dark eyes wide, distended and blazing with anger.

Ian caught her to him again.

"Fight—fight, my beautiful—it makes me want you more!"

"I hate you, I hate you!" Diana panted, then she gave a sudden scream, for with a single movement Ian tore her dress from neck to hem.

She beat him with her hands, but she was powerless against him. Her dress was thrown in a crumpled, tattered heap on the floor, and a moment later he lifted her high in his arms.

The firelight gleamed on the whiteness of her body and glittered on the gold of her tumbled hair.

She cried out, but there was no one to hear her, and, helpless, he carried her triumphantly into the shadows of the great bed.

Chapter 11

DIANA awoke to find the sun stealing into the room between the curtains, throwing shafts of golden light on to the dark floor.

For the moment she lay dazed, and then the memory of last night rushed back to her mind. Startled by it, she turned swiftly as she lay, but she was alone.

She lay still, feeling again the terror and horror of what had passed. She had fought until she could do so no more, and she had cried out until his mouth had stilled hers to silence.

It could not be true, she told herself. This could not have happened to her! But she bit back a sob as she knew that there was no mistake, and she was, indeed, lying here as much a prisoner as though she were handcuffed behind bars.

It seemed to her that by some trickery she had been transported to another century.

This vast room, generations old, was not the right setting for a modern girl, and she herself had been stolen, captured, and raped, as if indeed she were a woman of bygone centuries.

Wearily Diana rose, and walked barefooted towards the window and pulled back the curtains. She felt she needed air to help her to retain any sort of composure.

A rush of sunlight enveloped her, and as she flung open the casement the lap of the waves and cries of the swirling gulls came to her ears. Below her lay the garden, bright with flowers, and beyond was an emerald-blue sea, calm, but silver in its breaking against the yellow shore.

Far, far out she saw a ship, only a tiny streak on the horizon, and as it disappeared she felt like a shipwrecked sailor, watching the only chance of rescue vanish.

She turned from the window towards her looking-glass, and gave an exclamation at her reflection. Her hair was tousled and ruffled against her forehead, her cheeks were very pale and her eyes were ringed from the tears of the night before.

As she remembered those tears, she felt bitterly ashamed. She should have been proud enough to remain immobile, when she realized that her struggles would be of no avail; but she had pleaded and wept.

Diana sank for a moment on to the chair in front of the dressing-table, and hid her face in her hands, to jump startled to her feet as, with a faint preliminary knock, the door opened.

But it was nothing more terrifying than Margaret, with her early-morning tea.

It was after ten when she finally came downstairs, hoping, as she had refused breakfast, that Ian would have gone out, and she would be alone, with perhaps a chance of escape—but he was waiting for her in the Hall as she descended.

"Good morning!" he said, as gaily as if there were nothing between them.

She did not answer. Through the open door she could see a waiting car, and for the moment her heart leapt with the hope that he would let her go, only to have it dashed as he said:

"I thought you would like to drive round the island this morning, and we can ride this afternoon."

Sullen and discontented as she might be, Diana could not help noticing the beauty of their surroundings as they drove slowly along the rough roads, which were little more than cart-tracks.

After some way, Ian turned the car up the hill, and they finally stopped only a few yards from the great grey cairn at the summit.

"This is my grandfather's grave," he explained briefly.

Although Diana showed no interest, he told her a little about the old man, and how he had reigned supreme in his tiny kingdom.

Diana looked behind her, and saw the mainland for which she longed, and realized the impregnability of this island fastness. The distant peak of Ben Nevis might have been the gate of Paradise, so difficult was it for her to reach there unaided.

In spite of her misery, the island air whipped the colour back to her cheeks.

It was a lovely morning, and the scent of the heather around them and the salt of the sea were intermingled into a wonderful fragrance. A seagull mewed above them, white against a perfect sky, a cock grouse winged his way to the valley, a snipe startled by their approach, zig-zagged heavenwards.

From the fields below rose a stand of green plover. A trio of ducks, in perfect formation, flew by, on their way to a sapphire loch.

Yet Diana would not speak, and after a while they drove homewards.

Through luncheon she sat sulky and dumb, but Ian paid no notice. He talked occasionally, or sat indifferently silent, either action merely increasing her sense of futility.

Because she could not refuse, and there was nothing else to do, she changed after luncheon, as Ian had suggested, into riding-things.

Luckily, these had been included in her suitcase, for she rode when in Paris. A young Frenchman, who had loved her for many years, always put his stable at her command whenever she went there.

This afternoon it was too warm for her to need a coat, and in her silk riding-shirt and well-cut breeches she looked like a slim and beautiful boy as she mounted the magnificent grey horse that awaited her outside.

"When I bought Starlight," Ian said reflectively, "I thought he would suit you."

He himself was on a fine bay, which was pulling a little. But Starlight behaved perfectly, and Diana could not help being pleased at having such a mount.

They cantered away from the Castle, and then, on a smooth ride, gave the horses their heads. Over the ground they flew, the horses moving easily, the thud of hooves in their ears.

When at last they stopped, Diana was flushed and glowing, and, forgetful of everything but her momentary enjoyment, she cried out in happiness.

"That was wonderful!" she said. "This horse is marvellous!"

"I am so glad," Ian answered, but his smile made her remember where she was, and she rode on in silence, avoiding his eyes.

They skirted the marshes on the north side of the island, and turned eastwards until they were down by the shore. There were sands here, golden-brown and firm enough for a gallop.

About a mile along them there was a ramshackle hut built against the cliffs above high-water mark, appearing strangely insecure. Smoke was coming from its chimney, and despite her resolution not to speak Diana could not resist her curiosity, and remarked:

"What an extraordinary place to live!"

"That belongs to old Nanet Carmichael," Ian answered. "She is supposed to be a witch, and they think it is unlucky for her to live near the crofts, or even on the island itself; so she seeks shelter on the shore, where, according to superstition, bad luck cannot be perpetrated. They imagine, I suppose, it is washed away by the tide."

95

"Is she really a witch?" Diana asked.

Ian laughed.

"I have known her since I was a small boy," he said, "and, as far as I can make out, she is the only person who suffers from her bad luck."

At that moment they saw the old woman standing in her doorway, her hand raised to her eyes as she looked to see who was approaching. Ian greeted her.

"Hullo, Nanet!" he said in Gaelic. "How are you?"

"Sure, it's the Laird himself," she said, coming forward till she was within a few feet of him.

She was extraordinarily dressed, with bare legs and a short, tattered, and incredibly dirty kilt. Over it she wore an unbelievable number of blouses and woollen coats, surmounted by a torn shawl which had once been red.

Her hair, wild and unkempt, escaped from beneath a tam-o'-shanter. In her ears hung large cornelian earrings, and her bony old fingers were decorated with many rings.

She was a strange enough figure to make any misguided crofter believe in magic, and behind her, in the doorway of the ramshackle hut, were three or four skinny, furtive-looking cats.

"Your hut is still intact, I see, Nanet," Ian went on. "I thought the spring storms would have washed it away."

"Ay—ay, it is still there," she muttered, "but, dear knows, it was a hard time. There was plenty of driftwood afterwards, though . . . fine driftwood, from the ships that could not stand the storm like Nanet's house".

A wild cackle of laughter startled Diana, who could not understand what they were saying.

"A pretty lady," Nanet said to Ian, "pretty indeed —but she is causing you trouble, and heart trouble, too . . . I can see that, my fine Laird!"

She fixed Diana with dark, brooding eyes, and went

on mumbling to herself, so low that Ian could not hear. He thought she had forgotten them, and gethered up his reins, but before he could bid her farewell, she added:

"I see trouble for her too . . . trouble, indeed. . . ."

As if her gloomy prophecies had made her forget everything, she turned without a word and walked back towards her hut.

"What did she say about me?" Diana asked quickly.

But Ian did not answer, touching his horse with the spur so that it sprang forward, and with one backward glance at that strange old woman Diana perforce had to follow him as he cantered away along the sands.

Back at the Castle, tea was waiting for them, but before he had finished Ian was called away on some estate business, and Diana was left alone.

She wandered round the Library, looking at the contents of its oak shelves, and then inspected the Dining-Room, the Hall, and the Picture Gallery.

She had to be impressed by some of the treasures the Castle contained, however much she wished not to be; even her inexperienced eye knowing that the tapestry was priceless and that the wonderful carving in the Dining-Room was unique.

The pictures, too, of the Carstairs' ancestors were labelled with famous names, and must be worth a fortune.

There was a particularly charming portrait of Ian as a boy, by Sargeant, and another of the old Laird. Sargent, with his invariable skill and genius for portraying character, had never had a better subject.

The old man was standing, dressed in kilt and plaid, his dog beside him. There was wisdom, kindliness, and sincerity in his face, and yet the fierce Gaelic temperament was there too, and the power of a born ruler of men.

Twilight was falling before Diana realized it was nearing dinner-time, and she must change her clothes.

However, alone in her room, she did not undress, but paced backwards and forwards.

She felt it had been weakness to spend the day as she had, but there had been no other choice, and to remain in her room would not have carried her any further towards escape.

She had looked for a telephone, but there was none, and Ian had remarked that there was no post or telegraph office on the island.

She had instantly thought of the mail-boat, only to hear a moment later that Ian's own motor-boat fetched the letters twice a week from the mainland.

It was the same as being on a desert island—but, she had in fairness to allow, with the addition of a great many comforts of civilization.

If only the servants had spoken English, she might have been able to bribe them, though of that she was none too certain, for she was not blind to the obvious adoration they had for Ian. His servants, apparently, were his to command as unmistakably as if they had been his bought slaves.

Outside the Castle, everyone they had passed that day had curtseyed or saluted him, and their faces had lit up at his approach, as if he were not only their Laird but a friend.

Diana was no fool, and it had not taken her long to realize that Ian here was nothing less than a king among his subjects. If she were against him, it seemed unlikely that she would have the slightest help from any inhabitant of Ronsa.

She walked up and down, her hands to her temples, striving to think, until she found she had only ten minutes in which to dress. She had not forgotten that night was approaching, and that indeed was her chief thought as she went in to dinner.

She had even tried to make herself less attractive, putting on a severe black frock and dragging her hair back from her forehead. She wore no jewellery, and even left her rouge untouched, though she could not resist the temptation of slightly reddening her lips.

Had she but known it, she was even more attractive than usual. The severity of her dress threw into relief her white skin and the deep gold of her hair. Her pale cheeks accentuated the depth and beauty of her eyes.

Ian longed to ask her always to look like that, for the lack of ornamentation also gave her a less sophisticated appearance.

They sat silent through the meal that followed, Diana refusing to respond at all to Ian's conversation, eating fastidiously, as though the food would choke her.

In the Library they again took their places of the night before, Diana despondently on the sofa, Ian in the arm-chair, the dogs crouching affectionately at his feet.

"I want to write some letters," Diana said. "Have you any objection to them being posted from here?"

"Not at all—but I am afraid I must ask you to let me see them," he replied. "I cannot have wild bands of rescuers storming my island."

Diana sighed. She had been afraid that he would answer thus. Slowly the minutes ticked past on the grandfather clock which stood in the corner. Tick . . . tick . . . and every minute Diana felt that bedtime was nearing.

A log fell suddenly from the fire and startled her, but still they sat on in silence, only with the tick-tick of the clock wearing at her nerves until she felt she must scream.

At last she could bear it no longer. She jumped up, the soft skirt of her dress swirling round her with the abrupt movement.

"You asked me to marry you," she said, and her voice trembled a little. "Have you no heart? You can't do this!"

"My wife must be worthy of my home," Ian said,

99

and she felt the contempt in his voice as if he had struck her. "I would not marry you now. Besides, why should I?"

"If I were a man, I'd kill you for that!" Diana said vehemently.

"But you are not a man," he replied, picking her up in his arms. "You are only a very attractive woman."

And while she fought impotently against his great strength, he carried her upstairs.

Chapter 12

WHILE the rest of the island accepted unquestioningly any action of Ian's, there was one person who did not.

Jean Ross brooded over Diana's sudden appearance, and was not satisfied, without explanation, with her presence.

Jean, since her earliest remembrance, had loved Ian. She had adored him, as a sturdy, good-looking boy, when they played together, and when she saw him no more, memory only made her heart the fonder.

Starved for other companionship in the quiet life she led, and lonely at the University, where she made new friends, her only solace was in her memories of Ian.

She scanned the London papers for a mention of his name, and though she was seldom rewarded, she eventually collected a few meagre press-cuttings.

These she kept hidden in her box of treasures, which contained many curious souvenirs—a dirty, blood-stained handkerchief he had once lent her for a bleeding knee, a hare's foot from his first kill, the tail feathers of a woodcock, and several photographs.

These were mainly snapshots, generally indistinct and out of focus, but which, as an amateur photographer from her ninth birthday, she had once considered marvellous achievements.

Though Jean was pretty enough to attract the attention of men of Ian's class, she had little or no success with those of her own standing.

To begin with, she considered herself above them, becoming aloof and disdainful when they made any sort of approach to her, and also her vivid hair, which drew the attention of Southerners, was too usual among the labouring classes to be thought anything but commonplace.

She had made a few female acquaintances in Edinburgh, but she was a little shy of visiting their homes, feeling gauche and uncomfortable among their cramped gentility, and she was only too conscious of the deficiencies of her own home life to invite anyone to Ronsa.

A more adaptable girl, less self-conscious, would have suited herself to the better conditions around her, and taken advantage of them, but Jean merely withdrew into the shell of her reserve.

Therefore she remained lonely, unbefriended, for those long terms of the University—to return to alienate herself from her own people by an assumption of superiority.

Education of any sort was rare on Ronsa. Neither her father nor her mother could read or write, and no one on the whole island save herself could speak English. Little wonder that discontent rendered her moody and undependable.

She had intended, after her examinations, to seek a post on the mainland as a secretary, or school-teacher, but her mother was getting old, and just before her final examinations fell ill.

Jean was recalled, and when Mrs. Ross recovered it

101

was then too late, or maybe she was too apathetic, to start her studies again. Also, by that time she had become almost indispensable in the house.

No one on the island employed a servant of any sort, and it was obviously impossible for Mrs. Ross to continue the management and care of the household. And so Jean remained on in Ronsa, tied to the island, with no chance of any change except by marriage with one of the local farmers, which indeed would have made very little alteration in her life.

So, fed by repression, her childish love for Ian grew with adolescence into almost an obsession. When he was known to be in Africa, she sent to the mainland for every book she could obtain on that country.

She waded through geography books, books of travel, novels which, filled with dark-skinned heroines, made her weep bitter tears in case, held by the spell of another woman, he should never return again.

When the news of Colonel Carstairs' death reached Ronsa, conventionally though insincerely, the island inhabitants expressed their sorrow, Jean ran around, gayer than she had been for a long time, singing at her work, smiling at everyone, until even her father, usually unobservant, remarked on it.

And yet on the day of Ian's return to take up his position and enjoy his heritage, she had been unable to gather with the crowds at the quay and watch for the boat which would carry him across the water.

She had dressed in her best, as they all had, and started towards that waiting-place, but her feelings had overcome her, and she had slipped away into the fastnesses of the moor where they had so often played as children.

There she had lain face down in the sweet heather, thinking and dreaming fantasies which, in her heart, she knew would never come true.

Ian's call at their house, two days later, had inspired wild imaginings. Day after day she had waited for him to return, and when he did not she had shed bitter, despairing tears. She knew her love was an impossible, fantastic thing, yet she could not control herself.

It was part of her—grown up with her—until she could no more throw it out than she could withdraw her heart from her body.

"Ian—Ian . . ." She had whispered his name through many lonely nights, she had cried it to the winds on the moors, and she carried it hidden against her breast, written on the only note she had ever received from him.

Ian had been slightly wounded in 1916. It was nothing serious, but the whole island had been anxious until they were reassured by the old Laird himself that Ian was in no danger.

Jean had been in Edinburgh at the time, and had found the information in one of her many searchings through the newspapers.

For nights she had not slept, lying awake imagining him sick and untended. She had gone about her work white and shaken, until her companions had noticed it, and spoken to her kindly, for her misery was only too plain.

But she had hardly heard them, barely existing, until she finally received an answer to the letter she had written him.

It came one morning, when the students were all gathered round the porter, who was distributing the post, and she was unable to wait until she was alone before opening it. She had torn the envelope apart, and, when she read that he was well, had dropped down in a dead faint.

That friendly letter of thanks, crumpled and almost illegible now with many readings, had never left her, night or day.

On Ian's return to Ronsa, Jean would often neglect her work in the house, or rise so early that everything was done almost before dawn broke. Then she would wend her way the long miles of the Castle, and, hidden in the heather or lurking in the shadows of the pine trees, she would watch Ian drive past in his car, or see him exercising one of his horses.

It was a consolation for her aching love even to see him in the distance. She was humble enough to be thankful for that, even to require little more.

It was food, after so many years of starvation, to watch him and hope that she might have an opportunity of speaking to him.

Her heart warmed when she heard the Ronsa folk talking of him, every word bespeaking the great esteem in which they held him. She would never join in the conversation, but she would listen, her heart flowing with pride for the man she loved.

When she heard of Diana's arrival at the Castle, and in her spyings saw her at Ian's side, Jean was filled with a wild jealousy.

Few women had ever visited the island. The old Laird had occasionally entertained a house-party from the South, but his contemporaries were naturally elderly women, and Ronsa had never seen anyone like Diana before.

Her beauty and horsemanship were a revelation. Jean could not bear to hear her spoken of in awe and admiration.

Day after day, she hid near the Castle to see Ian and Diana ride by; day after day she watched them.

Sometimes they passed so near to her, as she lay crouched in the heather, that she could hear their conversation, and, with delight, she noted that Diana was sullen and uncommunicative, and that Ian seemed stern.

"Fool—fool!" Jean thought.

How could anyone look sad or cross in Ian's presence, how could anyone restrain from giving him their best?

And then, in spite of loyalty, there came whispers from the Castle of strange doings—"the lady was unhappy" . . . "she was practically held a prisoner" . . . "she spoke to the Laird with dislike and hatred in her voice". . . .

At first it seemed incredible, but then a closer scrutiny of Diana's expression led Jean to believe that it was the truth.

One day, in her interest, she forgot to be cautious, and ventured so near to the riders that Ian espied her behind a pine tree, and called her name.

"Hullo, Jean! This is a surprise," he said, reining in his horse.

Reluctantly, crimson with embarrassment, Jean stepped forward, ashamed of her rough clothes and untidy hair beside Diana's neatness.

"I was away to the Castle with a message from mother," Jean said quickly.

"Why—you speak English!" Diana turned to her, suddenly animated.

She had taken no notice when Ian spoke, hardly realizing that, for the first time in her presence, he was addressing an inhabitant of the island in English, but as Jean replied she was startled into the exclamation, and, checking her horse, she drew nearer.

"Yes," Ian said gaily, "Jean has been to Edinburgh, and has passed more examinations than I dare to think of."

"I am thrilled to find someone I can understand," Diana said eagerly. "I must come and see you one day, if I may."

Jean said nothing. The colour which had suffused her face had died away, leaving her very pale. She did not understand this sudden interest on Diana's part, and she regarded her nervously, uncomfortable, and uncertain what to answer.

"We will certainly come and visit you, Jean," Ian answered with an accent on the pronoun which did not escape either of the women, adding, to Diana: "Mrs. Ross makes the best hot scones in the world."

Diana ignored him. She still regarded Jean with eager eyes, but she sensed that this strangely attractive girl was antagonistic to her, and she wondered if she too were bound by the exaggerated devotion which affected all those surrounding Ian.

Jean was too overcome to be sensible of what she ought to say. With a muttered, "We will be glad to see you," she turned and fled.

Yet in her embarrassment first dropping the bob curtsey which the estate women had always performed to the old Laird, and which Jean had long since abandoned, considering her education had lifted her above such things.

As they rode away, Ian said to Diana:

"In case you are contemplating escape with Jean's aid, I can tell you she does not possess a boat or an airplane."

Diana tossed her head, and spurring her horse, galloped away from him without reply. But his words had put a new idea into her head.

An airplane! How silly she was not to have thought of it before! The shed was probably not kept bolted and barred, because there were not likely to be mechanical thieves on the island.

The hope and the zest of scheming cheered her up, and made her quite agreeable to Ian.

Jean had fled from their presence towards the Castle, but as soon as she was out of sight she retraced her steps, climbing upwards through the pine trees towards the moor. She was deeply conscious that she had shown herself to be uncouth and awkward.

Beside Diana's elegant refinement, she felt coarse and hoydenish, and she was filled with an overwhelming dislike of her.

She could not understand Diana's sudden interest, and she wondered about it all the way home; only as she reached the farm gate did light suddenly dawn on her.

movement. Jean could see that her shoulders were un-
covered, and her body barely concealed by a nightdress
of some transparent material.

Jean started to move from her place of concealment,
and was just going to call out when Diana spoke.

"There's nobody there," she said, and Jean was suddenly rigid, as a voice she knew so well answered:

"Of course not! Why should there be?" and Ian
appeared beside Diana.

He put his arm around her naked shoulders, and,
although she made a movement of impatience, he took
no heed of it.

Then Jean hid her face in her hands, for he drew
Diana close to him and back into the room.

Chapter 13

IT was a bright, crisp morning.

There was a slight chill in the wind, which was nevertheless invigorating, and heavy with salt, for it came
across the Atlantic and whirled round the Castle in little
whistling gusts.

It bent the corn in the valley, scattered the pine
needles, and blew Diana's fair hair into her eyes, as she
cantered leisurely on Starlight, accompanied by Ian on
his bay.

The sulky solemnity to which she had schooled her
expression, drooped her mouth and wrinkled her white
forehead in a slight frown, which was her only answer
to any observation her companion might make.

But she could not control the brightness of her eyes,

which came not only from the enjoyment of the morning but from perfect health and well-being.

It was no use denying that the ten days she had spent in captivity had done her good. Her fair skin was slightly tanned, but it was as clear and buoyant as the fulsome promises of the beautifying advertisements, to which she had so often lent her name.

Diana indeed felt well. Never before had she lived a life so free from the dissipation of late hours in a stuffy atmosphere, or the insidious continuance of cocktails and champagne.

Early to bed and early to rise was the rule on Ronsa, and if there were tiny violet lines under her eyes, they only added to her beauty instead of detracting from it.

There was no sign of fatigue in her movements, and she walked spiritedly, instead of moving with the slightly languid grace which was usual to her in London.

Never before had she owned to such an appetite, and in spite of her refusal to speak to Ian unless she were obliged, meals were enjoyable.

Diana had to own to herself that Ian was extraordinarily patient with her sullenness.

She did everything she could to goad him, even at times assuming an interest in his conversation, until he was undoubtedly carried away by his subject to enthusiasm and eloquence, and then with insolent deliberation she would leave him and the room.

Suspended half-way through a sentence, Ian would nevertheless good-humouredly shrug his shoulders, and remain altogether unaroused.

That in itself was galling to Diana's spirit—to find that apparently she had no power to move him save to passion, but there indeed he was not indifferent, her own coldness seeming to encourage rather than to dissuade him.

She had ceased expressing her hatred, for he only laughed and smothered her protests with kisses, so that she had learned to remain silent, hoping her very passivity would shame him.

During the day-time, Ian never attempted any embrace. She had nothing to fear from him until after the sun had set in a fiery blaze behind the long, rolling water of the ocean which surrounded them.

While they rode, drove, or sat together in the Castle, he was a charming, friendly companion whom she might have met in any house-party.

Ian had spent so many years alone that he did not need a listener to encourage his powers of conversation. So contented did he seem with this existence of one-sided pleasantry, that Diana almost despaired of ever convincing him of his execrable behaviour.

Riding now beside him, she glanced at him under her eyelashes, and saw how obvious was his enjoyment of the day. He, too, was bareheaded, and his shirt was open at the neck, showing a patch of white skin against the deepened tan of his throat.

He was smiling, as he turned to her to make some commonplace remark about the weather, and she could not help being aware of his good looks and fine bearing.

Few men of her acquaintance could ride as he did, seemingly part of the horse himself, and his horses knew of his love for them, and of his absolute fearlessness, so that—as animals always do—they trusted and loved him in return.

As they rode towards the hills, climbing steadily over the mossy ground, Diana saw that in the small harbour which adjoined the Castle a boat was putting out to sea.

It was not the usual motor-boat used for the mail, for that was painted white, and Diana knew it only too well, for every time it crossed and recrossed to the mainland it brought her a further sense of her helplessness and her inability to escape.

This boat was grey, and of different build, and dimly

in the distance she could discern a woman's figure standing in the bows holding the craft alongside, whilst a man prepared to go aboard.

She reined in Starlight, turning sideways to view the proceedings, and Ian followed the direction of her eyes.

"That's Jock Ross," he said, "and I think it's Jean with him. I wonder why he is going to the mainland. It is seldom he ever leaves the island, even for an hour."

Jean Ross, Diana contemplated . . . the girl who was so antagonistic to her, the girl to whom, she knew instinctively, she could, had she the opportunity, appeal for help.

"Let's go down and see them off," Diana suggested.

Ian, though suspicious of the pleasantness of her tone, agreed, and together they turned their horses and trotted towards the quay.

Jock Ross returned Ian's greeting cheerily, but Jean answered in a strange, defiant way that made Ian look at her in surprise.

"She's jealous," Diana told herself. "She knows or has guessed something, and she is jealous of him."

She watched Jean deliberately turn her back on Ian and busy herself with storing a few packages under the tarpaulin. She was looking extremely attractive, which, feminine-like, Diana did not fail to note.

She wore a kilt cut like a man's, and hung above shapely legs on which she wore no stockings, only short socks, and heavy brogues. Her shirt was green, and her tam-o'-shanter of the same colour framed her marvellous Titian hair.

Only her hands, rough from work, betrayed her humble origin. Otherwise, she might easily have been some descendant of a great clan, with all the attributes of fine blood running in her veins.

As she was moving about in the narrow confines of the boat, a heavy oar, which was shelved for use in

112

case of emergency, slipped and crashed into the centre of the craft, upsetting Jean's carefully arranged packages.

She struggled to raise it, but it had become lodged between the deck-boards.

In an instant, Ian had sprung from his horse, and lowering himself quickly into the boat was helping her. At his assistance, Jean's bad temper seemed to vanish. She laughed back at him, and, against her usual custom, spoke to him in Gaelic, so that Diana could not understand her or Ian's reply, and suddenly she felt infuriated that she should wait while Ian busied himself with this common girl.

Without a word, she rode off, turning Starlight towards the valley. Ian insulted her, she told herself, but this was indeed the last straw. She could not protect herself from his brutality, but she would not countenance his contempt before inferiors.

She whipped herself into a rage as she went, adding together the sum of her indignities until she was literally shaking with one of her familiar outbursts of temper.

Then suddenly she heard the thud of hooves behind her, and, turning her head, she saw that Ian was approaching, galloping swiftly after her.

In that moment the devil, which lurked in the temperament of all Stanliers, seemed to gain possession of her, and spurring Starlight she galloped away.

On and on she fled, her heart pounding with rage, her imagination conjuring this into an escape from all. She was evading her pursuer, freeing herself from Ian's tyranny.

She crouched low in her seat, whipping Starlight onwards until she saw that a large burn barred her progress, beyond which lay the cultivated land of a small farmer. So she wheeled up the hill, veering back towards the Castle.

Starlight was sweating, but going gallantly, and Diana

did not spare her whip. She realized she was leaving Ian behind, yet still she galloped on, faster and faster, the movement exhilarating her, her anger, like a black cloud, obscuring her reason.

She only knew that she must go on and on—that she must not stop. She forgot that she was on an island, she forgot that this was not escape . . . she only knew that Ian was behind, and that he was dropping back; she was escaping from him.

The incline down to the Castle was steep, but Diana did not falter. Through the pine trees, with dust behind them, they sped. Then she glanced around and saw that Ian was away on her right.

She had made a detour, and to gain the Castle stables she must turn towards him. He, having cut off a corner, would arrive almost at the same moment.

Perversely, she went straight ahead, and only when she saw before her the high grey stone wall which surrounded the grazing-fields did she realize she must rein in her mount, and submit tamely to enter the Castle as she had left it, with Ian beside her.

Then, with the wildness of unreasoning temper, she refused defeat, and swept onwards towards the wall.

Starlight slackened his pace, but Diana kept him on. "If I am killed, all the better," she thought, and put her horse at the wall.

Even as she felt him gather himself for the huge jump, a sudden doubt alarmed her.

The horse, game even against such insurmountable odds, jumped, but the height and the exhaustion of a long gallop was against him. Diana felt him touch the top . . . then she was flung through the air from the saddle.

She landed with a sickening bump, which slightly stunned her, but she rose after a moment unsteadily to her feet. She was dazed, but knew she was all right.

Then, with a shock which was photographed so vividly on her mind that she could never forget it, she saw what had happened to Starlight.

The beautiful horse was plunging madly, and Diana knew at once that he had broken his leg. Again and again he tried, but could not regain his feet.

He fell back, his head high, his eyes distended, and he gave a little whinny of fear. He was bathed in sweat, and foaming a little at the mouth.

"What have I done—what have I done?" Diana cried, stepping forward, but realizing she could not touch the horse as he struggled, his leg limp and useless.

"Oh, my God!" she breathed, unable to bear the pathetic sight.

She looked round wildly for help, and saw that a man was hurrying towards her, but before he could reach her she perceived Ian hurrying through a gate at the end of the field.

She watched him approach, fascinated. She was swaying on her feet, still shaken from her fall. She could never bear to see an animal in pain, and she could not look at Starlight.

His evident agony made her breath come sobbingly, but there were no tears in her eyes, only horror at what she had done.

Behind Ian ran the groom, who had evidently seen what had happened from the stables, where he had been waiting.

Ian galloped up, dismounted, and one quick glance told him, too, what had happened. He turned, remounted, and galloped back across the field. What was he going to do? Diana wondered.

Her teeth were chattering a little from the shock, and though the sun beat warmly on her head she was terribly cold.

The groom was at Starlight's head, talking to him all the time in a voice the horse seemed to understand, for he lay still, only with each muscle twitching as if he were in pain.

A few minutes passed, and Diana felt she had stood there for endless ages. She instinctively knew what the verdict would be, yet she prayed that it might not be true.

When she at last saw Ian coming back, she waited with her hands clenched to stop their trembling, only to know, when she saw what he carried in his hand, that her worst anticipation was correct.

As he jumped to the ground, he seemed to see her for the first time.

"Go back to the house," he said, and abruptly turned away from her.

Diana ran blindly as she was commanded, stumbling over the rough turf.

She never looked back, but she could not help hearing the single shot that rang out, echoing round the hill and back, until it seemed to her to boom endlessly on and on, ringing in her ears, its reproachful memory lingering long after, in reality, it had died away.

Upstairs in her bedroom she pulled off her boots with a jack, and took off her breeches and shirt. She had bruised the point of her shoulder in falling, and already it was slightly discoloured.

She was overcome by a great reaction from the temper which had caused all the trouble. She felt a little sick, and utterly miserable.

An abject depression seized her, and it was with difficulty that she restrained herself from uncontrollable tears. Starlight had been the one thing she had cared for since she came to Ronsa.

He could not persecute her, this dumb friend, with whom she had spent—almost, as it were, in spite of herself—so many happy hours. And now she had killed him!

Wrapped in her dressing-gown, she walked up and down her room, as she tried not to think what had happened, and to fight for self-control. And then, so suddenly as to make her give a little cry, the door opened and Ian entered.

His face was graver than she had ever seen it, and her heart gave a throb of terror as she realized, in looking at him, how angry he was.

She could find no words with which to express her sorrow, so she stood dumbly waiting for him to speak.

She had been facing the window when he entered, and she had looked at him over her shoulder, but one glance at his face had frightened her into looking away, so she waited with her back towards him for the anger which she could not but know she deserved.

His words, when they came, were spoken in a voice calm with a fury which was beyond the relief of any violent expression. Diana's temper, when aroused, shook her into an explosion of anger, but Ian's was quiet and bitter, and even stronger in its tensity.

"I would rather you had killed me than have done such a thing to one of my horses," Ian said; "and because you are apparently as irresponsible as a child you must be treated as a child."

With a sudden movement which found her utterly unprepared, he ripped the wrapper from her shoulders.

Only when she felt the sting of a whip on her bare skin did she realize, in the intolerable pain, what he intended to do.

Yet, after one low cry, she stood absolutely still, and received the following stroke without a murmur. It fell, cutting her with a physical agony, yet giving her a more intolerable mental humiliation.

She felt she could not bear another, and must scream for mercy, but as her breath came sobbing to defeat her pride, she heard the sharp crack as Ian broke the light riding-whip across his knees.

The two pieces were thrown at her feet, and as she stared stupidly at them through tears of pain, the door slammed.

She was alone.

Chapter 14

In her bed, Diana raised herself on one arm and listened. She could hear no sound, except the wind whistling round the Castle, and the moan of the waves.

All day, since that terrible episode, of which she dared not think, she had stayed in her room, refusing the food which had been brought her, only dreading nightfall, in case it should bring Ian to her again.

It was now nearly one o'clock, so she knew that he would not come, and that everyone else in the house must be asleep.

Born of her utter necessity for action, she had a plan of escape, a plan so desperate that even now in her frenzy she was awed by its daring.

Since the evening of her arrival at Ronsa, she had not seen her airplane. She had asked for it, but Ian had assured her it was safely housed, and that the mechanic who looked after his was paying every necessary attention to it.

With Ian almost constantly with her, it had been impossible to make any investigations for herself, but now that she was alone in the night for the first time she decided to attempt her escape, either in her own 'plane, or in Ian's, which was kept in the same shed.

The very idea was folly; no sane airman would have attempted such a flight, and she had had no experience of night flying. What chance could she have, with every condition against her?

She pictured in her mind the huge barn, with its corrugated-iron roof, which was used as a hangar for the airplanes. With a rising sense of hopelessness she remembered that the grass of the landing-field had not been cut.

Subconsciously, as she had hurried from the tragedy which had taken place there a few hours ago, she had noticed the thick growth of thistles and docks.

But she must not think of these things—she must escape! . . . She rose, and crossing to the window she gazed out into the night.

The clouds were high, and were moving rapidly. Would the wind also be in her favour? As she looked, a ray of moonlight stole through the clouds, and cast a silver glimmer on the sea. If only the night became clear, her plan might succeed!

She depended on the moon for light—the moon, Diana!—her namesake . . . surely Fate would help her!

Her only idea was to leave the Castle before she saw Ian again—however dangerous, she must, she would make the attempt.

The clock struck one. Her fire had almost died away, but she coaxed it with fresh logs into a feeble blaze which lit the room sufficiently for her to find her clothes.

Once or twice, as she hurried into them, her shoulders hurt her, but this, instead of hindering, only spurred her to greater haste.

She put on her leather flying-coat, slipped the helmet into her pocket, and, holding her shoes in her hand, very, very cautiously opened the door. In the passage there was darkness and complete silence.

She crept along, feeling her way with her fingers, until she reached the stairs. They creaked as she descended, and every time they did so her heart beat faster and she listened anxiously.

She decided not to attempt to open the front door, or the one leading into the garden, but instead to climb from the library window, which, on the west side of the house, had nobody sleeping above it.

She broke her finger-nails against the heavy shutters, but after striving with all her strength she managed to swing them open.

A moment later she slipped silently over the window-sill, dropped on to the flower-bed beneath, and walked away under the shadow of the wall.

It was hardly likely that anyone would be looking into the garden, yet nevertheless she was determined to risk as little as possible.

Once away from the house, however, she ran across the soft grass until she reached the gate which led into the landing-field. The rusty hinges squeaked as she opened it, and with a little gasp of terror she rushed on towards the shed, which loomed huge and dark in front of her.

She must get away, she thought—she must . . . almost panic-stricken by her fear; yet her brain worked clearly.

She remembered that she had never seen the front doors of the shed open, and therefore the mechanic must enter from another door, concealed somewhere in the building.

She was right—at the back she found a smaller door, and above it was a four-paned glass window.

The door was locked—she had expected that—but the window opened with an ordinary latch. It was out of her reach, and it took her some minutes to drag beneath the window some heavy logs, which had been stacked on one side of the shed.

When finally she was high enough to reach it, she drew a penknife from her pocket, and, inserting it deftly in the frame, after several unsuccessful attempts managed to lift the latch, so that the window swung open towards her.

She pulled herself up with her hands until she was half through the small aperture. In the dim light of the shed she could just discern the outlines of the two airplanes, each facing double doors.

Directly beneath her she could perceive nothing which might obstruct her entrance. With difficulty, but finally, with the only damage a torn stocking and a scratched arm, she was inside.

Her first task was to see if she could open the doors to get the airplane out. As she had feared, they were locked, and drawing the bars on the inside made no difference.

It took her some time to make a tour of the building before she eventually found a large key hanging on the wall beside a flying-coat and some overalls. It turned easily in the lock, and a moment later the wind swept into the shed, as she flung wide the first barrier which impeded her escape.

She had no electric torch, but the moonlight made it just possible for her to see her way about.

She knew there could be little petrol left in her tank —she must fill it herself, a task she had never previously done unaided. In a corner of the shed were a number of tins containing petrol, and beside them a small ladder.

Without wasting time, she started to carry the tins to the Moth, and when she had eight ready there, she dragged up the ladder and commenced to fill the tank.

Once she slipped on the ladder, and dropped a tin. The clatter of it resounded through the shed, and she feared someone must hear, but the silence outside remained unbroken.

She spilled nearly a can of petrol, but she did not wish to waste time fetching more, and she thought that once over the mainland she would find some place of landing where she could fill up.

She was so desperately anxious to be gone that she had no thought or apprehension for afterwards.

Her 'plane was too heavy for her to move unaided, but there was just room—though with only a few inches to spare—for it to taxi directly through the doors, once she had it started.

121

She had never started a 'plane by herself, and she had never swung an air-screw. However, she made the attempt, and pulled it round, but the throb of the engine did not greet her as she had hoped.

She advanced the throttle slightly, and tried again . . . again and again she strove, but without success, until she had to rest her tired arms and think of a further solution.

She began to consider logically. What could be wrong? Why should the engine not start? The mixture must be too strong, or too weak—but which?

It was too dark to see the engine, and it would only be possible for her to decide this vital point by smell, and if it were too weak, then she would have to flood the carburettor and turn the propeller half a dozen times to suck in a richer mixture. And if too strong . . .

It was all so complicated, and she was in no mood to think coolly of these technical points.

Then, suddenly, another idea crept into her head. Why should she bother about her own machine, if it would not start?

Surely Ian's 'plane would be ready—his mechanic would have seen to that. The thought gave her again a thrill of adventure, and brought renewed energy.

She turned to Ian's 'plane. It was a closed machine, a Puss Moth, and she had never flown one, but she thought she would be able to do so. Anyhow, she would take the risk, and, becoming reckless, she struck a match.

Below the wing she found the petrol gauge, and saw that the tanks were nearly full—surely Fate was helping her this time

With ever-increasing excitement, she flooded the carburettor and turned the propeller three times. Then she switched on, and with a final swing set the engine in motion. Success at last!

Quickly she removed the chocks, and, breathless with

apprehension and relief, hurried into her coat and climbed into the pilot's seat.

Cautiously she opened the throttle, and . . . the 'plane crept slowly forward!

Swinging inward, she cleared her own Moth, just missing the doorposts, and was out—taxi-ing across the field.

She taxied quicker, turned the machine into the wind, and opening the throttle eased the stick forward, and as the machine gathered speed, pulled it back . . . the 'plane did not rise.

To her horror, she saw she was approaching a wall which bordered the end of the field . . . she had only a few more yards to spare . . . still there was no upward movement.

Desperately she closed the throttle and swung the machine round . . . only just in time to avoid a collision, the machine, swinging round on its outer wing-tip, fortunately righted itself again immediately.

She switched off the engine. Why had she not been able to take off? There seemed to be no tangible reason. . . . She would try again.

This waste of time was exasperating. She listened, terribly afraid she would hear the sounds of someone hastening towards her. When she could neither see nor hear anyone, she climbed out of the cockpit.

She felt rather shaken, and her forehead and hands were damp with sweat. She wished she had some brandy with her.

How stupid she had been not to include in her preparations the silver flask which was in her dressing-case.

But it was easy to be wise after the event; she had dressed so hastily that she had not even troubled to take warm clothing—the wind bit through the satin of her jumper and chafed her legs, which were covered with cobweb-thin stockings.

She dared not waste much time, yet she was afraid. The nearness of her collision with the grey wall beside

her made her more cautious than she would have
wished to be, but already once that day the wall had
played a dramatic part with her, and she could not
bear the thought of another tragedy.

At last, desperate in her anxiety, she again started
the machine.

She taxied until once more she faced the wind, preparatory to flight . . . opened the throttle . . . eased
the stick forward . . . they gathered speed . . . she
pulled it back. . . . The machine refused to rise.

Desperately she dragged the stick back with all her
force, but to no avail. They sped across the ground,
and drew nearer and nearer to that inevitable wall.
Diana turned the machine, and switched off the engine, but it was too late.

The 'plane swung round, but the left-hand wing
crashed against the wall. . . .

The force of the impact was terrific, and for a moment Diana thought they would turn over, but the machine merely shuddered itself to a standstill, and she
climbed out, to see her last hope of escape lying shattered before her.

Only then did she realize that the drag caused by
the long grass had prevented the 'plane from leaving
the ground, and only then did the tears she had repressed break their control; and flinging herself on
the ground, she lay sobbing for a long time.

The grass was wet, but the rich smell of the peaty
earth came to her consciousness, and it was somehow
a little comforting.

She dug her fingers into it, her usual fastidiousness
gone. She felt so utterly alone, so desparingly miserable.

She wanted to be very young, to be lifted by tender
arms and held secure from everything which could
hurt her. Why had she ever grown up, to dread tomorrow?

A child lives only for today, it is happy or unhappy,

but there is never that gnawing apprehension of the future.

Diana's sobs died away, but she still lay half hidden in the high grass waving around her in the wind. Finally she pulled herself together, and walked slowly up the field.

There was still the faint chance that she could make her own airplane work, but she had little hope of that now. Forgetting her caution, she groped about until she found a box of matches and the stump of a candle, which she lit and carried to her Moth.

As she peered uncertainly into the engine in the dim light, she heard a footstep and turned to see Ian in the doorway.

Defiantly, though her eyes were swollen with tears, she faced him across the flickering candle. He was completely dressed, and she noticed he was breathing quickly, while with him were two of his dogs, panting as if they had been running hard.

He had obviously just come from a walk, and had not been to bed. He must have heard the roar of his airplane, and rushed to investigate.

He gave a short, disdainful laugh, slightly breathless.

"My dear child," he said, "you don't suppose I left your machine ready and waiting for you? It requires a good many hours' work before it is ready for flight."

And then he saw that his own airplane had gone. He stared quickly from the empty place to Diana, and back again, and Diana suddenly, with a weary gesture, blew out the candle and dropped it with a soft thud to the concrete floor.

"I have smashed your machine," she said wearily.

This was the second time today she had hurt something of his, and she wondered what he would do this time, feeling in her disappointment too tired to care.

"Smashed!" Ian echoed, and she pointed towards the end of the field.

He started away in the direction of her finger, and

she stood limply awaiting his return. She did not care what happened.

The excitement of the last half-hour, since she found her way into the shed, had exhausted her more than she could have believed possible, even on top of a nerve-wracking day.

She had one desire at the moment, and that was to sleep. Her whole body felt numb, her brain vacant.

When Ian returned a few minutes later, she was standing just as he had left her, only at his approach she raised her head, as if she anticipated his anger and feared his violence.

But she was taken into his arms, she felt her cheek against his tweed coat and his mouth on her hair and forehead, and heard him cry roughly, as he held her:

"You little fool! You might have killed yourself!"

Chapter 15

"LET me go!"

Diana spoke to Ian across the breakfast-table. He was just finishing his coffee, and looked up in surprise as she rose and cried out her plea.

As if trying to echo her words, the rain beat sharply on the window-pane, carried by a sudden squall.

For six hours it had rained, but now the wind was steadily rising, and there seemed in the lowering of the clouds and the grey sombreness of the sea the promise of a violent storm in the near future.

Already the waves were breaking fiercely against the low cliffs, sending fountains of silver spray into the garden, and their noisy roaring seemed to intensify Diana's depression.

Last night she had been too tired, too utterly weary, to talk or protest even, when Ian had taken her back to the Castle.

Docile, she had accepted the strong drink he gave her, and no sooner had her head touched the pillow than she had fallen into a heavy slumber.

She felt bruised and stiff, and it was very languidly indeed that she struggled into her clothes and came down to breakfast.

Ian had waited for her, although he had already been downstairs for over an hour. She answered his greeting, but after that ignored him, and it was not until she was somewhat revived by the coffee and food that she felt capable of coping with an argument.

She had meant to wait until they had left the breakfast-room, but the silence between them, combined with the elements, made her nerves, taut with fatigue, unable to bear the suspense.

It was with violence that she pushed back her chair, and said:

"Let me go!"

Ian deliberately finished his coffee, then rose to his feet.

"No!" he answered, his chin set determinedly. His expression and tone told her that his reply was no impulsive refusal given on the spur of the moment, but a decision obviously arrived at by thought and time.

"How long are you going to keep me here?" she forced herself to ask him quietly, for she had learnt from experience that hysterical outbursts were useless weapons against him.

"I brought you here for two reasons," Ian replied: "to teach you a lesson, and because I wanted you. My first purpose is obviously unfulfilled, and my second stands unaltered."

"I should have thought my punishment far exceeded the crime," Diana answered bitterly.

Ian did not answer, but looked at her, and the memory of her words to him that night in London when he had declared his love were intermingled with an image of Jack, as she had last seen him, pleading with her for her kindness.

And because she could not reply, she gave way to the irritation of her pent-up feelings, and stamping her foot she cried at Ian:

"All right—keep me here if you must . . . but for God's sake leave me alone!"

And as he left the room, she flung herself on to the low window-seat, beating the cushions with her clenched fists, in a very fury of frustrated anger.

Presently she sat still and stared out of the window. She did not see the falling rain or the grey mist which covered the usually lovely view. She only saw herself humiliated.

Had it been any other man, he would have disliked her, reproached, perhaps even insulted her; but Ian, without wasting words, had resorted to deeds, and while she hated him for it she could not but own that such behaviour, in the twentieth century, required courage and daring unparalleled in her experience.

Servants removed the breakfast, but still she sat there, gazing out with unseeing eyes. Then she was startled by a shadow on the window-pane, and the sharp tap of fingers against the glass to attract her attention.

Jean Ross stood outside. She was wearing a heavy mackintosh and a sou'-wester, but the wind had whipped her hair into wet strands against her cheeks, and the bare hand she raised to the window was blue with damp and cold.

Diana hastily opened the window, and the cold wind blew in with gusty violence, scattering papers, swing-

128

ing the curtains, and blowing Diana's hair about her forehead.

"What is it?" she said quickly, for she knew that Jean would not approach her in such a way except on a matter of importance.

"Do you want to go to the mainland?" Jean asked, and wild hope sprang up in Diana as she answered:

"Of course—but how?"

"I have the motor-boat," Jean replied, "below, at the Castle steps. My father is talking with the Laird—if you hurry, I can take you now."

"I shan't be a moment," Diana gasped.

She fled from the room, running upstairs as hastily as she dared. She met no one, and seizing her hat and coat and her bag containing money she rushed back to where Jean awaited her.

She clambered through the window with Jean's assistance, and a moment later, lashed by the rain and buffeted by the wind, she was hurrying down the narrow shingle path which led to the cliff.

Immediately below the Castle there was a small stone landing-place, seldom used, for the quay itself was only a quarter of a mile from the house. The steps, from disuse, were covered with seaweed, and the mooring-rings were rusty.

The motor-boat was there, rocking unsteadily up and down on the swell, and already nearly an inch deep in water from the spray of the waves.

It was one of the wide boats used in those parts for fishing. The motor was amidships, and more often than not flung oil on the passengers. The seats were greasy and smelt strongly of fish, but Diana was too excited to feel fastidious, and she crouched down in the bows, partially sheltered by a piece of tarpaulin.

Jean slipped the mooring, and pushed the boat away from the tiny pier. For a minute they rocked dizzily on the waves, as she cranked the motor; then a moment later they were away, rising and falling in the deep troughs of the ocean swell.

At last! She was free! Diana looked back at the Castle. She could see no one watching them: their departure had evidently passed unnoticed. Once on the mainland, she would realize what freedom meant, and savour the delicious triumph of her escape.

Then a sudden fear made her say to Jean:

"Is there a train?"

"There is one in thirty minutes," Jean answered. "I knew that when I came to fetch you. . . . It is the only one of the day."

She was shouting above the throb-throb of the engine and against the wind which tried to blow the words from her mouth.

Diana was quickly soaked to the skin. Every foot of progress was fought for with difficulty, for they could make little headway in such a sea, and the tide was against them.

However, the Castle slowly faded into the distance, growing grey and indistinct, till finally it was swallowed into the mist, and in front of them loomed the rough outline of Torvish harbour.

Shivering, but elated, Diana stepped ashore. They had succeeded, and she—she had escaped!

She could have sung with joy, even though her teeth were almost chattering with the cold and the damp, and her fingers were numb, for she had forgotten her gloves.

She turned to Jean with a smile, and held out her hand.

"I can't thank you enough," she said. "I don't know why you should have done this for me, but I am so grateful."

She was standing on the steps of the quay, and Jean was facing her, the motor-boat held steady by two men who had come to the assistance of their landing.

"I helped you because I wanted to get rid of you," Jean answered.

Diana was taken aback by the harshness of her tone, and the dislike she saw in the girl's face.

"He is too good for the likes of you! You wanted to go, and now I have given you your opportunity. You don't like Ronsa, and Ronsa doesn't want you!"

She spat the last words at Diana, and before the latter could recover from the surprise of this outburst Jean had shouted a command to the men who held her mooring, and was turning the boat out of earshot.

Diana hurried up the narrow street to the station—there was no mistaking the way, for it stood a hundred feet or so above the harbour, the signals visible to her like flags of welcome.

Torvish was only a tiny hamlet of a few scattered fishermen's cottages, a post-office, and a small kirk, but it boasted a station and a lifeboat, and therefore was the principal social centre around for many miles of that sparsely inhabited country.

There were groups of people gossiping outside the post-office, who stared curiously at Diana, and she found at the station a large number waiting for the train.

Some were journeying farther up the line, but most of them were expecting delivery of goods, for the railway acted as a local carrier, the roads being a much longer and more devious route of transport.

Old men wrapped in shabby plaids smoked clay pipes as they waited, women with shawl-covered heads held animated conversation in Gaelic, or shouted pleasantries to the housewives of neighbouring crofts.

A thin, agitated girl held a few-weeks'-old baby in her arms, a wicker basket containing food, and a bulky bundle of clothes.

Another mother, laden with provisions, had three small children whom she kept beside her with difficulty, scolding and screaming at them, as they ran around, getting in everyone's way, and impeding the only station truck as it was wheeled laboriously down the platform.

One and all regarded Diana as if she were an inhabitant of Mars. Damp and dishevelled, in her wet coat and drenched felt hat, she was nevertheless too smart for this desolate place.

After a prolonged scrutiny, tongues began to wag again, but voices were lowered, and the topic of their conversation was evident.

Diana was told at the booking-office that the train was going to a small junction up coast, where she would be able to change on to a main line. Ten minutes later she was seated in an ancient and stuffy carriage, en route once more for her own world.

The first part of her journey was comfortless and exasperatingly slow. Diana still felt insecure. Ian seemed so invincible that she could not believe she had defeated him.

Alone in that empty carriage she sat, rigid, oblivious of her clothes, too nervous to relax, too apprehensive even to powder her face, until they arrived at the junction.

Only when she was warm and comfortable in the swift express which was carrying her South did she really feel safe. But physically she was wretched and fatigued, and she arrived in London feeling ill, and with a bad cold.

As she drove through the streets, it seemed years since she had seen them last, years since she had hurried through them that bright morning to Hanworth, looking forward to her holiday in the South.

She felt immeasurably older, and as though everything familiar was not so much part of her as it had been.

It was strange, and she was different; yet even while she thought, she tried to laugh at herself for letting her imagination deceive her. It had all been a nightmare which she could easily forget—she had escaped, she would not allow Ian to enter her life again.

She had no intention of telling anyone of what had happened. She was too ashamed and humiliated by the memory of it.

She wanted only to take up again the normality of her own life, to gather her friends and her amusements around her, as it were for protection, not against him but against herself and her memories.

All night in the train she had lain awake, unable to escape from her own thoughts. Once she had fallen into a drowsy unconsciousness, only to awake suddenly in startled terror, as she fancied that Ian was beside her.

With a sigh of relief she had sunk back on her pillow, only to imagine that the rumble of the wheels was saying.

"Are you really free? . . . Are you really free? . . . Are you really free?"

Over and over they repeated it, until she asked herself the same question—was she really free? Could she ever escape?

She had believed in her power—where was that power now? She had thought that no man could consider her other than in adoration and reverence.

Could she face the world with the same assurance, could she ever again have confidence, or rally herself to courage and intrepidity, while haunted by the memory of her utter degradation?

Ian had conquered not only her body but her spirit; she could still fight, still defy life, but her courage was undermined. Would not the memory of those ten days in Ronsa remain indelibly with her?

She was home.

The taxi drew up with a jerk at the door, and in answer to her ring a startled footman opened the door for her to enter the dustsheet-covered and shutter-closed hall.

Without a word, Diana ran up the stairs, past her own room, until at last she reached Ellen's door, panting and breathless.

She rushed in. Ellen was sitting in her usual chair, sewing. At least she was unaltered, and everything about her was the same.

The dear, familiar room. Ellen's smile of welcome, her outstretched arms . . . and suddenly Diana, unable to speak, was sobbing, while the familiar hands and voice soothed and comforted her, as they had so often done before.

Chapter 16

VIOLET LONGDEN had a villa high above the Corniche Road, overlooking Cap d'Antibes.

She had decorated the villa, which had an unusually beautiful garden, in modern cubist style, which somehow suited the flagged floors and the rough white walls of untouched stone.

Diana found a double welcome, on account of her delayed arrival, and was not surprised to find that all her usual friends were present, and quite unsuspicious that her unpunctuality was due to anything more than a prolonged orgy of gaiety in Paris.

It was extraordinary, she thought to herself, that one could disappear completely for over ten days without anyone being the wiser, or in the least anxious.

Rosemary Makines was there with Leadhold, and Ronald, in his usual way, was amusing himself and everyone else.

There were several other men, most of whom Diana knew well, and two or three young married women without their husbands, escorted by attendant cavaliers, who were apparently a permanent fixture.

It was curious how easily hostesses fell into the way of inviting a pretty married woman with her young man, instead of with her husband.

In fact, the Americans, anxious to make no mistakes, had an extra visiting-list they headed "couples". A few husbands and wives certainly appeared on the list, but they were generally the more old-fashioned sort, and were not invited to any but the more formal parties.

For the south of France, or for intimate dinners, it was far more convenient to invite two people who were attached only by affection; it simplified the arrangements of the table, and made the party a success, because one knew immediately who cared for whom.

Violet Longden declared publicly that her villa was barred to married couples.

"They have no idea of fair play," she would say, "and while the woman invariably takes someone else's young man, I have to amuse the husband—which, I may add, generally ends my friendships with the wife —while Johnnie indulges in another of his sulks."

There was no doubt that Violet "coupled" with Johnnie Nicholson.

He was a good-looking man of thirty, with a hatred of any sport more arduous than bridge, but with a lazy charm of manner which endeared him to most people, even while they despised him for living on Violet's considerable income.

Hidden away in America, Violet had a husband, who, according to all reports, adored her. Certainly, on his brief twice-yearly visits to his wife in Europe, he seemed contented enough with his extraordinary matrimonial arrangements.

But the few people who had met him had a vague memory that he was somewhat pathetic.

However, he apparently admired the social laurels Violet collected in London, Paris, and the Riviera, and then, having admired, he returned to grind out the dollars that she might triumph further.

Someone once asked Johnnie how long Mr. Longden's visit would last, and the answer was:

"Until he has read all the press-cuttings."

There might even have been some truth in the assertion, for Violet had every journalistic mention of herself collected and bound in books of purple calf, inscribed with her name and the date.

The number of these books had already reached two figures, and they were housed on a special shelf in the villa, in a cabinet in Paris, and in a carved gilt whirligig in London.

They travelled with Violet under the care of her secretary, whose business it was to keep them up to date, and even to add a few flattering remarks under the snapshots and studio-photographs included in the volumes.

There was much speculation among Violet's friends as to who would receive this precious collection on her death. She had no children to be thrilled with "Mummy's exploits".

Rosemary insisted that they would be left to the British Museum, but a rival hostess suggested, somewhat maliciously, that the waiting-room of the "Girl's Encouragement Society" would be more appropriate.

Violet was quite aware that her friends laughed at her, and that she was often criticized severely, but her large bank balance made her position too secure for her to mind.

They might sneer and condemn, it made no difference; they would fawn upon her, come to her parties, and solicit her generosity.

Though Diana, through her birth, was a feather in Violet's social cap, she was also genuinely fond of her. She had even tried, unsuccessfully, to marry her to one or two of her special favourites among the young men who thronged her drawing-room, wherever she was in residence.

Violet had little use for the unmarried state, in spite of her cynical convictions. She considered an absent husband was an effective background, and she was too worldly wise not to realize that Diana's reputation was suffering from continual gossip over each successive flirtation.

This season she had a new protégé to introduce to her. He was of one of the oldest families in France—a charming man, cultured, with a delightful manner and a fascination for the feminine sex which few women could resist.

That he was impoverished, accounted, of course, for his singleness, for even today a rich Frenchman is generally affianced in his teens to a *parti* chosen by his parents.

Violet had great hopes that Antoine de Sélincôte would appeal to Diana. Like most Americans, she had the match-making complex. Johnnie chaffed her when she unfolded to him her schemes.

"I thought you were fond of Diana," he said lazily.

He threw back his head and let a cloud of smoke out of his mouth.

"Of course I am; you know that Diana is one of my dearest friends," Violet said.

"Then why seek to exclude her from our society— anyway, from here?" Johnnie asked. "Your marriage ban," he added, in response to Violet's frown of uncomprehension.

"Diana will be different," Violet said; "and a French husband is so sympathetic."

Johnnie laughed.

"I think it most unlikely, that Diana will achieve successful marriage where so many have fallen by the wayside. However, have your own way, my love. You would, in any case!"

Diana's arrival speedily put an end to Violet's plans.

She was obviously not only disinclined for marriage, but also, most unusually, disinterested in men.

As it happened, Diana disliked Antoine from the first moment she met him. He was short, and she disliked short men. He was affected, and she hated affectation. He was insincere, and she loathed insincerity.

She dismissed him from her thoughts in the first hour of their meeting, and Violet good-humouredly resigned him to her already large collection of unwanteds.

As a matter of fact, Violet and the rest of her friends at the villa were puzzled by Diana's behaviour.

At first, she had seemed unusually gay, anxious to rush hither and thither at the slightest provocation, more impetuous than the best of them, craving for gaiety with an appetite which seemed almost insatiable. In fact, to them she was her normal self, slightly more effervescent than usual.

And then, after a day or two, she had seemed suddenly to weary, disdaining even the slightest exertion, refusing to join in any of their occupations, preferring to stay alone in the garden of the villa.

There was a hammock erected in the shade, and there she would lie hour after hour, not asleep but daydreaming, her eyes gazing unseeingly into space.

Even Ronald failed to rouse her with his good-humoured chaff, and when, more seriously, he attempted to make love to her in his inimitable way, she had bade him be quiet, and risen imperiously, to wander indoors.

It was Rosemary who tackled her at last, one night when they were preparing for bed. Diana was leaning over her balcony, clad only in a chiffon nightgown and a light wrap, when Rosemary called out from the doorway.

"Come in, Diana. I want to talk to you."

Diana obeyed with an obvious lack of enthusiasm. She dropped on to her bed, half sitting, half lying against the mass of lace pillows which Violet provided for the comfort of her guests.

"What is it?" Diana asked.

Rosemary rearranged her dressing-gown of peach satin in the glass before she sat down, surveying with pleasure the slim silhouette of herself against the cream walls and green hangings of the room.

"What is the matter with you?" she asked.

"The matter?" Diana echoed. "Why should there be anything the matter? I don't know what you mean, Rosemary."

"Don't prevaricate, my sweet," Rosemary answered. "I know you far too well for you to pull that innocent stuff over me. You're changed since you came down here, Diana, and we all know it. Ronald is miserable, and even that stupid Johnnie has sensed that something has altered you. Come on—tell me!"

Diana stared at her for a long moment before she spoke, then her answer came as a surprise, even to herself.

"The truth is," she said, "I've come to the conclusion you are all incredibly boring."

Rosemary jumped to her feet.

"Good heavens!" she said. "You must be sickening for something! I have never heard such an assertion in my life—especially from you, Diana!"

She walked a few steps across the room, then turned and pointed an accusing finger at her recumbent friend.

"You're in love!" she said. "Don't deny it—I know the symptoms far too well."

"I'm not!"

Diana sat up and glared at Rosemary with such ferocity as to render her friend speechless.

"I'm not," she continued after a moment's silence. "How dare you say such a thing? I've never been in love in my life, and I hope to God I never am. I want to be alone now. For heaven's sake, leave me in peace!"

And Rosemary, overcome by this outburst, walked towards the door. She passed through it, and was just closing it behind her when she turned back and laughed.

"I think you protest overmuch," she said slyly, and shut the door with a reverberating slam.

Alone, Diana walked to the window. She felt she needed air, but the warm night only seemed to envelop her as though it were cotton wool; she could not formulate, even to herself, the thoughts that were in her mind.

She wanted to straighten the maze of her feelings, and shelve her emotions as she always had before. Invariably she had been able to catalogue every feeling and to put it away, labelled, on the shelf of her memory, forgotten until she needed it again.

But now, since she had left Ronsa, she had felt as if she were on a roundabout—round and round went her thoughts, the circle of their speeding never widening, never narrowing, only remaining a chaotic whirl, dazing her and making enjoyment impossible.

Never before had she failed to appreciate the gaiety of this particular company of friends, or to find them untiringly entertaining.

Yet at the moment she loathed the thought of visiting the Casino with them, of dancing, even of bathing in the still, blue sea from the warm beach of golden sand.

She was restless, and yet at the same time she wanted to be alone, to lie tranquilly in the shade, undisturbed by the life around her.

As long as she could remember, she had always been the leader; in whatever set she had found herself, it was Diana who suggested—Diana who planned—Diana who arranged—Diana whose imagination provided the unusual, even for the most surfeited fun-seekers.

Yet now Violet and her visitors waited in vain. Diana would acquiesce politely and unspiritedly in their plans, or drift away from them before they could stop her, seeking solitude and peace alone.

One afternoon she was lying in her favourite hammock, when Ronald approached noiselessly towards her over the grass. She did not hear him come, and for a moment he stood looking down on her, as she gazed at the branches over her head.

She was wearing a colourful jumper and trousers, but her arms were bare, and she remained untanned, in spite of the fashion for bronzed beauties.

It was hot, and she had pushed back the curls from her ears, giving her a strangely youthful look. Her dark eyelashes were accentuated by faint lines of sleeplessness, yet her lips, slightly parted, were red and inviting.

Only hesitating for a moment, without thinking of anything but her beauty, Ronald bent over her, and kissed her on the mouth. Diana started violently, and then to his utter astonishment burst into tears.

"Darling!" he said. "Don't—please don't! I had no idea I should upset you. Don't cry, Diana—I can't bear it."

Genuinely distressed, he tried to wipe away her tears with his handkerchief, but they only flowed anew.

"What is the matter?" he begged.

He realized this flood of unhappiness could not be entirely due to his action. He had often kissed Diana before, though not for a long time.

At last the tears stopped, and Diana, realizing his distress, gave him a watery smile.

"I am a fool, Ronald," she said, "just a fool!"

"Let me help you," he begged.

"You have," she answered, "you have been very sweet. Thank you!"

"Look here, Diana," he said impulsively, "you're fed up with this crowd. That's obvious. And so am I. Marry me, and let's get away from everything. We'll go anywhere you like—Timbuctoo, or the Zambesi River —it doesn't matter. I will try to make you happy, and even if it doesn't succeed eventually, let's have a sporting chance at it."

Diana smiled; yet she considered what he said. She was unhappy, she was bored, and she did not know why.

All she realized was that she could not take up her life again where she had left it. Things which before had pleased her, she now found tedious to a degree. People who had made her laugh, now made her yawn to a point of exhaustion.

She wanted to go away, she wanted to forget herself. Perhaps Ronald was a solution—she did not know. He was so fond of her, so obviously concerned by her unhappiness—it seemed to her a long time since anyone had minded about her.

She was tired of everything. She only wanted to be comforted, consoled, to be made a fuss of. She wanted tenderness, not passion—she wanted the protection of someone as maternal and loving as Ellen, but at the same time she was feminine enough to need a man.

Ronald, kneeling beside her with his arms around her, anxiety in his eyes, seemed to comfort and relieve for a moment her utter depression. They would go away, right away, from everything.

Wearily, she supposed they must be troubled with the formality of marriage, but once that was over he would keep her from everything harmful—"From Ian," she added quickly. Even he could not touch her then.

With a little sigh she dropped her head against Ronald's shoulder.

"All right, let's get married," she said. "But, oh, Ronald, let it be soon!"

Chapter 17

THE house-party received the news of their engagement with varying emotions, but all were with one accord unanimous in their surprise.

Rosemary was distinctly peeved. Although Ronald

was in love with Diana, he had found Rosemary a charming companion, and she had made considerable and continual use of him as an escort whenever Lord Leadhold was not in attendance.

Violet had never thought of such a contingency. Ronald had been in love with Diana ever since she had known him—that was to be expected—but that Diana would accept his proposal had never entered her wildest dreams.

Ronald was too stereotyped, too obviously only one of a majority, for her to anticipate that Diana would single him out.

She could have understood Antoine, or anyone unusual, attracting Diana, but for her to marry someone so ordinary and commonplace was a shock.

Violet took so long to recover that she nearly missed the opportunity of explaining, not very convincingly, that everything was the outcome of her own special plans.

The engagement was, of course, not to be announced until Lord and Lady Stanlier returned from America; but gossip in the Riviera spreads so rapidly that within a few hours almost everyone along the coast was cognisant of the true state of affairs.

Ronald was naturally in the seventh heaven of delight, but Diana received their congratulations and enthusiasm with a quietness which puzzled even her dearest friends.

In spite of Diana's and Ronald's protests, Violet insisted on giving a celebration party, and as money can work miracles, it seemed a mere second before she had transformed the garden of the villa into a ballroom.

She laid a parquet floor, hung lights from every tree and shrub, but cleverly left the walls and roof to Nature itself, to the velvety, warm night, which no man-made masterpiece can ever attempt to rival.

She had decided that the dance should be in fancy

dress, and everyone telegraphed to Paris, or rushed hot-footed into Cannes in search of suitable apparel.

Rosemary, of course, fancied herself as a Rosetti angel, and indeed her costume of pale green was particularly effective. Johnnie, in spite of all opposition, insisted on coming as a Russian Cossack, for which he had neither the size nor the figure.

Violet's dress was kept secret until the last moment, when she appeared as a glorified Cleopatra, literally dripping with jewels from head to foot.

Only Diana did nothing to procure herself a dress, and Violet was so horrified when she found out her intention of appearing in ordinary clothes, that she and her maid set to work to garb her as a Snow Maiden.

On the night she looked so lovely that her home-made dress easily eclipsed the expensive productions which had been expressed from Paris.

She was tightly swathed in white chiffon glittering with diamond dewdrops, and it fell in fold upon fold into a heavy train of snowy ermine powdered with silver frost.

On her head, also borrowed from Violet, she wore a huge Russian tiara of diamonds, and her arms and neck were covered with the same jewels on bands of frosted ermine. Two long plaits of tiny pearls fell, medieval fashion, from her ears, and a cap to match hid her own hair.

Ronald fell in with Violet's suggestion that he should be a foil for Diana's splendour, and he wore merely the white uniform of an Austrian regiment.

They looked a wonderfully handsome couple as they stood beside Violet, receiving the guests who flocked to the villa, only too eager to be present at any shape or form of party, especially Violet's which were noted for their lavishness.

They came from Cannes, from Monte Carlo, from everywhere along the coast, driving up the Corniche Road, their headlights flickering through the darkness, their horns and voices awakening the silence of the night.

The music from the band in the garden echoed over the whole hillside; drifting away, joined in harmony to the wind with its burden of fragrance from the many flowers.

A magnificent supper awaited the merrymakers on the terrace. Violet, with true American hospitality, spared no thought or cost in her efforts to please. The inevitable champagne was not enough. There were liqueurs of every sort, and rare hocks and clarets for the discerning.

The villa itself was arranged so that every room held corners and nooks for couples seeking privacy. On the swimming-pool, which was at the bottom of the garden, were tiny gondolas, which drifted to and fro, unmanned save for fairy lights at bow and stern.

It was nearly midnight before the guests had ceased arriving, and Diana was already tired with accepting good wishes, though Ronald became more elated with each fresh congratulation.

Diana felt she was living in a fairy-tale. The whole setting of the party was so unreal, the motley collection of bedecked people, dancing madly under the stars, the stimulus of love, wine, and food making them oblivious of everything around them except themselves.

They could not see the stupidity of this extravagance, the foolishness of money poured away with little appreciation from anyone.

Violet's guests were here because everyone else was here. They enjoyed themselves because they knew everyone else was saying it was enjoyable. They were not grateful to her, only to the chance that got them invited.

They took the food and drink as their due, and Diana knew that, had it not been so perfect, they would have grumbled and complained.

Few of them would bother to thank their hostess more

than perfunctorily for their evening's entertainment, when they left, and none of them would give her a thought, were they not anxious she should amuse them another time.

Diana danced with Ronald.

"My sweet!" he whispered. "You are looking too lovely."

Diana smiled faintly.

"A Snow Maiden!" he added. "Will you melt?"

Diana could not reciprocate his gay mood, or reply lightly. She gave a little forced laugh, but did not speak.

Then, before she could refuse, he had led her swiftly from the dance-floor, down a pathway bordered with shrubs. This Violet had tactfully left unlighted, and a cushioned seat under a large tree was a perfect place for lovers.

But Ronald did not sit down. He took Diana in his arms and sought her lips.

"Darling!" he murmured over and over again, his breath coming quickly.

"You'll make me so untidy . . ." Diana pushed him away from her, but Ronald would not be checked so easily.

"Please, Diana—sweetest, I love you so! I adore you —I want you, Diana—let me!"

"Leave me alone!" Diana spoke sharply.

Then, as Ronald stepped back in surprise, she added hastily, "I'm sorry—I didn't mean to be cross, but I've got a headache."

Ronald was instantly all consideration and sympathy.

"I'll get you some champagne, darling," he said; "wait here."'

The moment he had gone, Diana disappeared in the opposite direction. She found her way to the cliff's edge, where a wild profusion of shrubs and bushes made a perfect hiding-place.

Ronald would not find her here, and if a loving couple

passed, she knew her white dress was visible in the darkness, and they would naturally imagine she had a companion with her.

Alone, she pulled off the heavy tiara. She was tired, and her head was truthfully aching. Why had she done this? she wondered. It was unkind to Ronald. Did she really want to marry him? she asked herself.

Ronald would protect her, and she knew she was afraid of being alone, yet doubts came creeping into her mind—doubts of him, doubts of herself, and grave doubts for the future.

How long she stayed there she did not know. When she left, she made a circuitous route to the house through the back way. Before she could join the dancers again, she had to readjust her headdress.

She went upstairs to her room, but, once there, she made no effort to hurry her return. The music of the band and the laughing chatter of many voices came through her window invitingly; but she sat at her dressing-table unheeding, hardly hearing the gay noise.

She was remembering another dressing-table at which she had sat not so many evenings ago. The huge glass had reflected her, and beyond her the corner of a great four-poster bed.

This glass, gilt and ornate with flowers and flying cupids, imaged her likewise, with the glory of borrowed diamonds against her neck, and the bizarre effect of pearls framing her face.

But behind her was no great four-poster, with memories to make her wince and shrink, only a single bed covered with green taffeta.

What had Ian done after she had gone, Diana wondered—had he sought her in that huge, austere bedroom?

What had he done with her abandoned belongings—the bright dresses she had left hanging in the vast cupboards, the clutter of gold brushes and intimate things she had left lying around?

Quite vividly, she could see him standing there, his face showing no emotion as he realized what had happened, only his broad shoulders squared, his chin set as it did when he was thinking seriously.

She had learnt to recognize the almost imperceptible signs which told Ian's mood for the moment. When he was happy, when he was excited, and—she shuddered at the memory—when he was angry.

The slightest change in the eyes, the line of the mouth, the movement of the hands—how well she knew him! Diana thought, and yet again, how little she understood him.

She supposed Jean had told him what had happened. Would he be angry with the girl, Diana wondered, or would he accept the obvious compliment of her love for him?

The thought of Jean's final words made her drum her fingers in angry irritability on the dressing-table.

She had never replied to that surprise attack. She had had no answer ready. Her cheeks flamed in anger to think she had been beholden to such a woman.

She would rather—she thought—have remained there, Ian's prisoner, than have accepted with gratitude such assistance. Anyway, it was too late now; what was done could not be undone. Doubtless Jean would find her reward in Ian's arms.

She disliked the thought. Ian, in spite of his faults, was too fine a man to be caught by the scheming of an uncouth farmer's daughter.

Yet Jean was attractive—even Diana could not deny her that—and who else was there on that lonely island to rival the spell of flaming hair, with temperamental love, already his, only awaiting his word?

Why must she think of all this—why—why? Diana wondered. She sprang to her feet, and seizing the tiara placed it again on her head.

Her looks did not please her—she dabbed rouge on

her cheeks, and reddened her mouth, yet still she knew she did not appear at her best.

The flashing diamonds seemed to make her lifeless—they not only took the colour from her cheeks but the light from her eyes. She contemplated her reflection ruefully, then with a shrug of the shoulders walked towards the door.

"What does it matter?" she asked herself. "Does anything matter? Oh, God! I wish I knew what was wrong with me."

She went down the stairs. There was a pause in the dancing, and couples were sitting everywhere. She replied perfunctorily to the chaff and gaiety with which they greeted her.

Rosemary was furiously angry. Lord Leadhold had spent the whole evening with a Columbine. No one seemed to know who she was; but she was very attractive, with perfect legs, and a dimpled, laughing face suitable to her costume.

Rosemary had interrupted them several times, and insisted on dancing with her "old boy"; but no sooner did she leave him, than he was back again with the girl, and now they had disappeared together.

Violet, her arduous duties of hostess having abated a little, sought Johnnie, to find him very intoxicated and noisy, so she was displeased; while Antoine de Sélincôte, having taken someone else's "sweetie" in a gondola, was engaged in a wordy war, which might end at any moment in a fight.

Altogether, the house-party were not enjoying themselves.

As Diana came downstairs Ronald appeared in the doorway.

"Where have you been?" he exclaimed. "I have been looking for you everywhere."

"I don't feel very well," Diana answered.

"My poor darling!" he replied. "Come and sit down for a moment, and I will get you a glass of champagne.

I got you one before, but drank it myself. What you need is a drink—you will feel much better after it."

He found her a seat on a sofa in the sitting-room, and hurried away to the buffet.

Diana leant back for a moment, then restlessly she bent down to take from the fender-stool at her feet one of the papers which were arranged there in neat, stereotyped rows.

The first one she took up was, to her surprise, the *Scotsman,* a paper she had not expected Violet to have in the house; but she saw the reason for it when she found inside a picture of Violet herself, with the announcement that:

"For September, Mrs. Longden has rented one of the best-known forests in Inverness-shire."

If that was for Johnnie, Diana thought with a smile, the stage would have an extremely quiet season; but a moment later she remembered that Mr. Longden was expected on one of his short holidays, and guessed that Violet intended to beguile him with better entertainment than usual.

He had nothing in common with the gossiping crowds in the Riviera. Languidly she turned over the pages, and then a photograph made her start.

It was of Ronsa Castle. How well she knew those pointed turrets with a centre tower. There was her bedroom window; there beneath, the portion of the garden through which she had sped just seven days ago.

Then she gave a startled exclamation, as she read the legend beneath:

Castle Ronsa, the ancient and beautiful home of Mr. Ian Carstairs, whose gallant rescue of the victim of a motorboat accident is described on the opposite page.

Diana found the column, and, hardly able to hold the paper steady for the trembling of her hands, read:

AVERTED TRAGEDY IN
THE WESTERN ISLES

A motor-boat piloted by Miss Jean Ross, the daughter of one of the tenants on the Ronsa estates, capsized in the heavy gale which swept the islands on August 10 last. The cross-current and tide, combined with the force of the gale, caused the boat to be swamped, and Miss Ross would have lost her life had not Mr. Carstairs, the Laird of Ronsa, swum to her rescue and kept her above water until the Torvish lifeboat could come to their assistance.

At the time of going to press, Mr. Carstairs is undergoing medical attention for the injuries he received, but Miss Ross has completely recovered.

Then followed a long description of the island and the Castle, but Diana did not read any more. She was trembling from head to foot, and the paper had dropped to the floor.

She knew with a sudden clarity that unmistakably and irrevocably she loved Ian.

Chapter 18

THE Blue Train, once it had left the twisting coast behind, sped forward at a tremendous rate.

Diana in her carriage with its shining orange walls leant back comfortably against the grey velvet-covered seat, and stared out of the window at the rapidly changing landscape.

The hurry of her departure had left an impression only of many tongues gabbling and chattering at her, of disapproving, astonished faces, and protestations which were drowned in the general hubbub.

Only Ronald's face, as he pleaded with her, was vivid. She had been sorry, she had felt almost maternally tender towards him, but her decision remained unaltered—the engagement was broken.

From the moment she had read of Ian's injuries, she knew there was only one course open for her, and that was to return to England immediately.

The knowledge of her love for him revolutionized herself and every other consideration. Ronald must be cast aside, the others could think what they wished; she did not care.

They had all begged her to consider before she acted so hastily. Violet had spoken even more severely—she was concerned not only with Ronald's happiness but with the endless explanations the Riviera would require of such conduct.

They had received the congratulations and good wishes showered upon them last night, had seemed happy and contented, and now, five hours after the party ended, without a moment's notice, the bride-to-be was packing, having announced that the marriage would not take place!

"How can you be so heartless?" Violet had argued. "You always were selfish, Diana, but this is beyond everything! What can I say—how can I explain? And, after all, what has poor Ronald done that you should treat him like this?"

"Nothing," Diana said briefly. "I have told you that. Ronald is unaltered, just himself—it is I who am changed."

"But how can you be changed in a few hours? You

are absurd, Diana, and I will never forgive you—never! The whole affair will cause endless gossip."

"Until the next scandal," Diana said wearily.

She was collecting together her things as she spoke. She was dressed, and almost ready for departure; while Violet, aroused from her bed, was tousled from sleep, or rather the lack of it, for the party had not ended till long after dawn.

"Won't you give me some explanation?" Violet said, trying to control her ill-temper. "Tell me, anyway, Diana dear, why you must leave like this. . . . Stay here! Ronald won't bother you, I promise, but don't rush away before we have time to think, or even to grasp what has happened."

"I have said all I mean to say," Diana had answered. "You can hardly expect me to break off my engagement to Ronald and remain under the same roof, can you?"

"There's something behind it all," Violet declared; "I know that. You can't deceive me, Diana—I've known you too long. But what, God knows; and I am too tired to guess, at this moment."

Her departure from Diana's room had only preceded Ronald's arrival. He had already argued with Diana for a long time, and had left, only in the hope that Violet would succeed where he failed. Now, despairingly, he tried again.

"If only you would tell me, Diana—what have I done?"

"Nothing! I have said 'nothing' till I am sick and tired of saying it!" Diana cried. "I've told you, I've told Violet, I've told Rosemary, I've told everybody that it's nothing to do with you. Let's leave it at that!"

Yet now, sitting in the train, she reproached herself. She was sorry for the boy, and at the same time she knew she could never honestly have contemplated marrying him.

It had been a moment's madness, and that longing

for protection was due more to physical fatigue than to anything else.

And Ian? Her mind raced at the thought of him. . . . How was he? . . . Was he better? The paragraph in the paper had been written over a week ago—he would surely have recovered by now.

It was her fault, and bitterly she blamed herself. She had heard of the tremendous currents round Ronsa, and there was no doubt that when she left Jean the storm was getting rapidly worse.

Fool that she was to have accepted that horrible girl's invitation to escape, and it had cost her dearly, for now she knew that she loved Ian, and she had severed herself from him more completely than by any other barrier. He might forgive her for everything but that Jean's life had been endangered.

Whatever she touched seemed to go wrong, Diana thought bitterly, especially anything connected with Ian —first Jack, then Starlight, and now Jean, had not Ian himself stopped the malignancy of Fate.

At last Diana realized why she had disliked Jean from the first moment she had seen her. She was jealous of her, jealous of Ian.

She must in reality have loved him for a long time, but her absurd pride had kept her from realizing it. Truly her vengeance had returned to herself like a boomerang!

She thought of Ian, and the picture of him, so strong, so virile and compelling, brought her suddenly the realization that he was lying sick and ill, his magnificent strength laid low. Who was with him? she wondered.

Perhaps Jean had recovered sufficiently to nurse him —she could pour out her love, and who knows but Ian would return it?

With miserable humiliation, Diana told herself that Ian had never loved her since the night she had spurned his proposal.

He had wanted her—yes!—but he had treated her only as a light woman, desirable for the moment.

There had been no tenderness in his passion, none of the sweet love-making which mattered so much more to a woman than anything else. Ringing in her ears came his words: "I would never marry you," and the bitter ending ". . . why should I?"

How could she have been so blind when she first met him? How could she not have understood that here at last was the man she had waited for all her life?

No wonder other suitors had found her cold and aloof. They were not worthy to be called men beside Ian—and yet, when she found him, even when he had loved her, still she had not understood.

Regrets could not help her now, nothing that had happened could be altered. How she had failed him, and how terribly she had failed herself!

She saw herself now as she was—spoilt, intolerant, taking everything from life and giving nothing in return—and of her knowledge of Ian, she knew the type of woman that he held idealized in his heart.

She remembered so well, just after she arrived at Ronsa, he had taken her on a tour of the Castle. She had gone with ill grace, sullenly, refusing to speak; but he had ignored her humour, and shown her everything, in spite of her lack of interest.

He did not prevent his pride in the wonderful place bespeaking itself in his words and in his voice.

They had entered at the end his own rooms, very simple, furnished only with absolute necessities, obviously the rooms of a man who was used to wide spaces, and hated a clutter of knick-knacks about him.

The walls were panelled, but over the mantelpiece in one of his rooms there hung a large picture of a very beautiful woman. Painted by a great artist; the whole figure seemed alive.

The eyes were looking into the room, the mouth just parted as if about to speak. It was a face not only lovely in feature but the expression also revealed a fine character, intelligent, sympathetic, and of absolute sincerity.

Diana had stared at it, and finally curiosity had overcome her sullenness.

"Who is that?" she asked.

"My mother." Ian had answered.

She had remembered then that in London he had told her of his childhood and how the loss of his mother when he was so young had coloured his whole existence, and that never had he forgotten her.

It was the only picture, and the only photograph, in his bedroom. No other woman in Ian's life could rival her—and yet she, Diana, had once been paid the greatest homage he could offer any woman.

She knew that Ian had never loved before, and that, if he wanted to marry her, it meant that he considered her perfect enough to share a place in his heart with the mother whose image had remained so vivid all through his life.

After Ian had said, "My mother", he had turned abruptly and led the way from the room, and that remembrance added now to Diana's bitterness, for she knew that he had not cared to speak of his beloved mother to a woman whom he despised.

Why indeed should he marry her? Ian had not been carried away by a pretty face. He had believed in her, thought her ideal, when he had at last proposed. And then, when she had revealed herself in her true colours, his love had vanished, leaving only passion.

As the train rushed through the fields and villages of France, Diana faced the bitterest moment of her life. She had always had what she wanted, but now it was too late. She had thrown away her opportunity, and she saw little chance of another.

And then, suddenly, a wild idea came to her. If he

would not love her, at least she could live with him again. Surely he still wanted her. . . . With a rising heart, she remembered those nights she had found so hateful at Ronsa.

Hateful! She laughed bitterly at herself—dear God! Give her the chance of them again!

She knew now her restlessness, her boredom, her utter depression since she left Ronsa, had all been due to her aching want of Ian. She wanted him—she loved him, every moment away from him was unreal and lifeless.

She must see him again, she must be held close in his arms. She would make him love her again, she would try to restore that fallen ideal of herself.

Surely the task was not impossible; surely if she could once return to him she could show him how different she could be. Every look, every word, every hateful deed she had performed in his presence, came back now to haunt her and to jeer at her unhappiness.

She saw herself spiteful, ill-tempered, unreasonable —and, in her own love, she at last understood how terribly she had made others suffer.

This aching torture . . . this misery . . . this want of someone unobtainable . . . this was what Jack had experienced. He would be sorry for her now, she thought, he would understand her, and at last she understood him.

Haggard with sleeplessness, Diana finally arrived at Victoria. At Grosvenor Square she found a cold welcome. Ellen was laid up, and the servants were bored and impatient that their holiday must be interrupted by her continual reappearances.

They were not expecting her, and there was nothing to eat. However, Diana had no interest in material comforts. Her maid repacked her luggage as quickly as she could, discarding the elaborate pyjamas and thin dresses, which Diana had required for the South, for heavy tweeds and warm clothes.

Within two hours of her arrival in London, she had left again, and was travelling rapidly northwards.

She knew she was behaving in an unprecedented way, but her whole relation with Ian had been unusual. If she could lower her pride, and return to him—and she was prepared to return on her knees, if he asked it—surely he would receive her.

She expected nothing; she asked only that she might return to the Castle as his mistress. Time and her own dear hopes might bring her the happiness she begged.

Mixed with her misery was anxiety for his health. Recklessly, she bought every Scottish paper; but, bar the first information she had found in the *Scotsman,* she could learn nothing further.

She did not wire of her arrival, caution telling her that somebody else might open the telegram, and, apart from that, there was the dread that he would refuse to take her back.

In the sleeper she lay thinking of him, for sleep was impossible. How terribly she loved him! And she knew, now, why she was not alone in her adoration, why everywhere he went Ian had friends; how could she ever have been his enemy!

She acknowledged, to herself, that it was his greatness which had so swamped and dwarfed her little world, that he had come into her life like a tempest. She could not at first grasp the grandeur and magnificence of him.

Instead, she had pitted her puny strength against him, and had failed. He had conquered her, and she was glad of it, but the knowledge of her gladness had come too late.

Once her pride had gone, she saw how it alone had kept her determinedly antagonistic to his compelling charm. She knew now that the happiest time of her whole life had been the month they had spent together in London.

She must have been mad to suppose that her enjoyment of those dinners together, and those days of perfect companionship, had been due to the advancement of her cheap revenge.

They said that love was blind—certainly hers had been. She must really have loved him then. His presence had contented her, and his first kiss had thrilled her. When he had finally proposed, he had spoken to her as she had never heard him speak before or since.

At Ronsa, his voice had often been deep and moved by passion, but that night in her sitting-room in Grosvenor Square there had been an emotion so beautiful that it was almost reverence.

There had been worship in his eyes, which ever afterwards had been replaced by burning desire or contempt.

"Ian—Ian!" Diana cried into the darkness.

If only she could undo the past—if only she could start again from that night he had knelt beside her!

But her voice was drowned by the noise of the wheels that, like Fate, she thought, ground on and on, carrying her into a future of which she was afraid.

Chapter 19

THERE was a Scotch mist which blotted out everything beyond a distance of a few yards from her eyes when Diana stepped out of the train at Torvish.

It was cold, with a penetrating dampness, and even

her thick tweeds could not prevent her feeling chilled and miserable by the depression around.

She had planned to hire a motor-boat at Torvish, but this was not so easy as she had thought, and she waited over half an hour in the rough shelter of a wooden shed before one could be found to carry her to Ronsa.

The island was quite obscured by the mist, and it seemed to Diana as though it were a bad omen, that she could not even see her longed-for destination.

The shelter, which contained a battered boat and a number of fishing-nets, kept out the damp, but not the cold. Finally, in desperation, she opened one of her boxes, which had been placed beside her, and wrapped a fur coat around her.

Men entered, from time to time, seeking this and that, or—as Diana thought more probable—curious for a glimpse of her, but she could not speak their language, and beyond an interested glance they left her severely alone.

At length the chug-chug, of an engine told her that the porter had been successful in his search. She tipped him handsomely, and she longed to ask him if he had news of Ian's health; but she was frightened that he, thinking she knew nothing, might not wish to arrange her passage without the Laird's permission.

Ian was so omnipotent here that Diana knew that were these people to get the idea that he was not expecting her, they might easily refuse, whatever inducement she offered, to carry her to the island.

The boat was a small and somewhat dirty one, and the fisherman a dour old man of sixty years or so.

They stowed her luggage away, leaving her a tiny space in the bows, where she sat bolt upright on the hard seat, twisting her head as they went, to obtain a first glimpse of the island, until it loomed dull grey through the fog.

They had landed at the little quay before she could see even the outline of the Castle. There was no one about, and the owner of the motor-boat merely placed her luggage on the stone landing before taking her money and disappearing into the mist.

As the noise of his engine died away, Diana turned and walked slowly towards the Castle.

Now she had arrived, she was more nervous than she had anticipated. She was frightened of what reception she would find, of what news she would learn of Ian. The mist around her, with its unreal silence, seemed to envelop her mind, as well as her body.

At last she reached the gate into the garden, which was the quickest way from the quay. The shrubs and trees were dripping heavy drops of moisture, and the flowers, which must have been beaten down by a recent storm, lay across her pathway, and, as she touched them, dropped their wet petals against her legs.

She did not dare to enter the house by the side door, but went round to the front and pulled at the heavy bell. She heard it ring far away, and then, after what seemed to her an eternity, footsteps came slowly to the door. One of the men-servants opened it, and looked astonished at her appearance.

She walked past him into the house. The great hall was dim and silent, but a huge fire burned in the grate, and Diana went gratefully towards it, holding out her cold hands to the welcoming blaze. She turned to find the man evidently waiting for her to speak.

"The Laird?" she said in Gaelic, remembering those two oft-spoken words of the strange language.

He pointed upstairs, and then hurried away from her, evidently to announce her arrival.

Diana stood a long time in front of the fire. She listened, but could not hear voices, or anything except the crackle of the logs and the tick of the great clock.

When her patience was almost exhausted, and her nerves frayed with anxiety, she heard footsteps, and looking up saw a nurse descending the stairs. Each steady footfall resounded on the oak, combined with the rustle of her starched apron.

She drew nearer and nearer, but Diana could neither move nor speak; she could find no words to express the question which hammered in her ears and cried aloud in each rapid beat of her heart.

The nurse therefore spoke first, speaking in the matter-of-fact, refined voice of her profession.

"I understand you have come to see Mr. Carstairs."

"How is he?" Diana's voice came in a whisper.

"He is better, but the Doctor has ordered him absolute quiet, and, I am afraid, no visitors."

Then, seeing Diana's consternation, she added more kindly:

"He received several injuries to his head, you know, which have caused him to suffer from violent headaches, after his first delirium had passed. A very bad concussion, of course, and also he broke an arm—but that, I am glad to say, is well on the way to recovery."

"How terrible for him! He is really all right—there is no danger?"

Diana spoke these words with difficulty, she was so frightened, so terrified something was being kept from her.

"He is quite out of the wood, I am glad to say," the nurse answered brightly, "but I am afraid that you cannot see him. The Doctor will come again tomorrow, of course, and perhaps you can . . ."

She hesitated. She was going to add, "come back again." Then, remembering the desolate surroundings of the island, she substituted a question for her original words.

"Are you staying in the neighbourhood?"

"No, I have come back to stay here," Diana said determinedly. "My name—I am sorry I forgot to introduce myself—my name is Diana Stanlier. I left only on the day of the tragedy, and returned as soon as I heard what had happened."

The nurse looked rather nonplussed. That she had not heard of Diana before was quite evident, and she was naturally surprised that a strange and very beautiful young woman should arrive and announce her intention of remaining in a bachelor household.

Diana sensed that there might be some opposition, and quickly added:

"I have left most of my clothes here, anyway—I had every intention, of course, of returning to fetch them, but not so soon."

"Oh!"

The nurse again seemed at a loss for words. Her quick glance had espied that Diana wore no wedding-ring, and, feeling unable to cope with the situation, she rang the bell.

"Shall I send for Margaret?" she suggested, and Diana thanked her politely.

"This is a most unusual case," she added confidentially. "I have never before been in a house where the servants only spoke Gaelic. Luckily I know a few sentences, otherwise my task would have been very difficult. As a matter of fact, the night nurse, who is with me, comes from these parts, and speaks far better than I do. Otherwise I should find great difficulty in getting everything I require for my patient."

Now that she had accepted Diana, it was evident that she was only too pleased to find someone to talk to. The days were long while her colleague slept, and she had no one with whom to chat.

Margaret came hurrying, and through the medium of the nurse Diana was able to arrange for someone to fetch her luggage from the quay. Margaret was obviously none too pleased to see her, for she greeted her with only dour looks, but luckily she vocally gave no expression to her feelings.

"I suppose everyone here blames me for what has occurred," Diana reflected ruefully.

Margaret dispatched, she turned to the now friendly nurse with the inquiry: "How is Jean Ross?"

"Oh, she's quite well. She escaped with only a few bruises, and, of course, her constitution is so strong she suffered no ill effects from shock. She has been up every day to inquire for Mr. Carstairs."

"Has she seen him?" Diana could not help asking, and the nurse gave her a swift glance of suspicious curiosity, before she answered:

"Of course not. I told you Mr. Carstairs has not been allowed any visitors."

Diana hoped the relief she felt did not show in her face, she was so terribly glad that her fears were unfounded. Jean therefore could have progressed no further, in pursuit of Ian's affections, since the day she had left her, speeding back to him in the motor-boat.

Upstairs, her room was just as she had left it, but instead of finding it a prison she welcomed it as eagerly as if it were her home. There were her things, as she had left them; there the bearskin rug before the fireplace and there the great four-poster. . . .

Had she only known, she thought, how precious it would seem to her now! Instead, she had loathed and shrunk from the thought of it, dreading its comfortable embrace.

It was tea-time before she had changed her dress, and washed away the grime of the journey in the soft, peaty water which filled her basin.

Tea was laid in the sitting-room which held so many memories. The night nurse had awakened now from her sleep, and she was introduced to Diana by the first nurse, whom she now found was called Sister Williams.

"This is Sister McLoed," she said gaily, and a fat, cheery Scotswoman rose from a chair with extended hand.

"Is it Miss Stanlier?" she asked.

"Lady Diana," was the answer, and they both regarded her with renewed interest, for the name seemed vaguely familiar, having—as they afterwards remembered—so often found Diana's face and doings in the gossip columns of the papers which they read on duty and off.

There was plenty of conversation over tea. Diana found it a little wearying. They had all the artificial brightness which is part of the medical psychology.

They were intensely interested in their patient, and in Diana's connection with him, and, striving to be nice, they regaled her with detail after detail of different cases they had attended, all more or less nauseating to the layman.

Sister Williams was not Scottish, but had taken her training in a Glasgow hospital, and was now permanently attached to one of the great northern nursing-homes, from which, with Sister McLeod, she had been summoned by Ian's doctor.

They treated Diana to a lengthy description of their journey, and the scene which awaited them on their arrival. The whole population of the island was standing, weeping, outside the Castle door, they said; and, obviously, they took no little credit to themselves that they had been chosen to nurse so important a patient.

"You have never seen such a doleful set, and they greeted us as if we were a miracle come to save him—which we have, of course," added Sister McLeod with a cheerful grin.

"I am sure you have," Diana said gratefully.

"It was a hard task—I am not deceiving you on that," said Sister McLeod. "He was in a bad way, and I can't say I got much peace for the first night or two."

"I was never off my feet in the daytime," said Sister Williams, not to be outdone in this description of endurance. "But he is all right now—he will be himself in a week or two. But concussion is a nasty thing, and he kept living over and over again that rescue."

"He was worried about it?" Diana asked quickly.

"He had got it fairly on the brain," was the answer. "Even now he wakes screaming in the night. It's lucky your room is so far away, Lady Diana, or it might disturb you."

Diana said nothing. There was a lump in her throat, and her eyes, as she bent them low over her cup of tea, were full of tears.

Not a word about her . . . if there had been, she would have known it, for they would have shown no surprise at meeting her. It was of Jean he had thought in his delirium, her rescue haunting him.

At that moment the object of her thoughts was announced. Jean Ross strode into the room, dressed in her kilt, her head bare and her red hair sleek from the damp atmosphere. She greeted the nurses with a cheerful "Good day", and then she stopped dead, and her expression changed as she saw Diana.

"You back?" she said harshly before anyone could speak.

Diana rose, lifting her eyebrows slightly at this unceremonious greeting. Her breeding enabled her to pull herself together quicker than Jean—besides, she had known that they must meet sooner or later.

"Good afternoon, Miss Ross," she said with ironic courtesy. "I am glad to see you have recovered from your accident."

Jean walked slowly across the room, until she stood facing Diana. She was a head taller, but Diana, drawn to her full height, was far the more dignified of the two.

"Why are you here?" Jean said grimly.

"I believe this is Mr. Carstair's house," Diana answered quietly. "I have returned as his guest."

"He has not asked you—he has been too ill to ask anybody. You have no right to come here! It is your fault he is ill—your fault that he nearly died. I should never have attempted the crossing on such a day if I had not been anxious for you to be gone!"

In her anger, Jean relapsed into a broad Scotch accent, rolling her "r's" with all the ferocity of a Gael moved to violent expression. The two nurses had risen to their feet at this extraordinary outburst, and it was Sister Williams who stepped forward and laid a firm hand on Jean's arm.

"Come, come, Miss Ross," she said sharply. "Lady Diana had left her luggage here, and had returned for it. I think you must be a little overwrought—you are still not very strong, you know."

Jean shook her off impatiently, without turning her head.

Diana was standing with a disdainful smile on her face, her head thrown back, her smart clothes a vivid contrast to the other's rough dress. She raised a white hand with pink-tipped nails to smooth her hair from her forehead, and to touch for an instant the perfect pearls which hung round her neck.

Then, scornfully, she regarded the overheated Jean, to turn to the astonished nurses with a deprecating smile.

"I am afraid the accident has upset Miss Ross," she said, but Jean interrupted her again.

"You think you can come sneaking back here while he is ill—because you are a lady, and I am only a farm girl on his estate! But you don't love him—and I do! I won't have you here, I tell you—when you left before, I told you what we thought about you on Ronsa! We have no use for fancy ways and fancy behaviour. We are plain people, and the Laird is one of us!"

She would have said more, but Sister McLeod took her firmly by the shoulders, and propelled her forcibly, though she protested, from the room. As the door shut behind them, Diana sank down on the sofa, shaking a little and unnerved.

"Dear me—dear me!" said Sister Williams. "How very upsetting! What an extraordinary young woman!

I think she must be a little unhinged—I am so sorry this has happened, Lady Diana."

Diana, in spite of herself, could not help smiling. Right or wrong, she realized that the two nurses would be on her side.

Already she guessed they were fancying romance, planning a wedding, and only too eager to help such a nice-looking couple into that doubtful state of bliss.

Sister Williams was murmuring what were intended to be consoling explanations of Jean's behaviour. Diana knew that the nurse imagined she had superseded Jean in Ian's affections.

The only course for her narrow mind was to suspect that Ian had enjoyed liberties with the farm girl, while she, of course, was different—to be led a blushing virgin to the inevitable altar.

"If this well-meaning fool only knew!" she thought. "How the truth would scandalize and shock her!"

Impatient under the soothing words, not daring to contradict Sister Williams, yet hating the deception, Diana rose and hurried to her bedroom.

Alone, she flung herself face downwards on the bed, hiding her face against the pillow where Ian's head had so often rested.

Chapter 20

DIANA awaited the Doctor the next morning, and when he had finished examining his patient he regarded her inquisitively, as he sipped the glass of port which Margaret brought him.

He was a round, fat little man with a heart of gold, though his practice showed him little of that currency.

He was an extremely clever practitioner, and noted for his skill and for his kind heart over the whole of the Western Isles. He had known Ian since he was born —in fact, he had brought him into the world one sunny May morning.

He had tended, until his death, the old Laird, who had regarded him not only as his medical adviser but also as a friend.

Seldom a month passed when he did not spend a night at the Castle, telling the old man the local gossip, and enjoying a game of backgammon, which he invariably lost.

He was a bachelor, for he always said that no woman could stand the uncertainty of his life, or cope with the fact that he might be home tomorrow, or a fortnight later.

Storms would sometimes maroon him on one of the outlying islands, but not often, for he would brave almost any weather to go to an ailing patient, or to deliver another sturdy Scotsman into the world.

The doings at the Castle before Ian's accident had reached his ears, as surely as all gossip of the Islands did sooner or later, and he had promised himself that he would pay a surprise visit to find out the truth, only to be circumvented by the urgent summons of Ian requiring his professional attention.

He loved the boy, and it had been a shock to find him so ill, and through the long hours of anxiety he had muttered Scottish curses on the head of the woman who was responsible; but face to face with Diana he found himself unable to be angry with her.

She was so indisputably beautiful, and—a keen judge of human nature—he knew immediately that she was in love with Ian. That Jean was the same way inclined, he had known for a long while, and he saw

169

the humour of the situation, even while he was anxious as to what would be the outcome.

He was not sure what were Ian's feelings in the matter. He was only conscious in snatches, and during those times he had not mentioned Diana, his delirium bringing him only memories of the rescue, and how he had battled against seemingly impossible odds to save Jean's life and his own.

He must surely be in love with this beautiful girl, the doctor thought, and yet again he was uncertain.

Ian was very like his grandfather. The old Laird had been loved by so many, and in return only cared for one woman in his life.

Margaret had meant no disloyalty to Ian when she had told the doctor of Diana's visit, of quarrels, disagreements, and silent meals at which neither spoke.

At first, the doctor, hearing of Diana's unchaperoned visit, had anticipated that he would meet a peroxided chorus girl, or one of those unattached women with a none too savoury past.

But one glance at Diana told him he was mistaken. Here was a thoroughbred, and when he heard her name he imagined that he was merely old-fashioned not to realize that the bright young things of today required neither protection nor chaperones.

"He's bad, lassie," he said over his port, "but he will be all right. You needn't worry unduly. The boy's got the strength of ten ordinary men."

"Can I see him?" Diana asked eagerly, but he shook his head.

"Not for a day or two," he said finally. "He mightn't recognize you, and if he did it's ten to one it would send his temperature galloping—which, if I may say so, would not be surprising," he added gallantly.

Diana thanked him with a little smile.

"And it's no use your moping for those days," he continued. "They won't pass any the quicker if you do. Go out and take some exercise—ride all his horses,

170

but don't break your neck. I've enough trouble on my hands as it is."

He was surprised at the vivid flush which swept over Diana's face at the mention of riding. He did not know that the thought of Starlight made her utterly ashamed.

"Well, I must be off," he said, rising. "I have a patient at the end of the island, and a queer one indeed. Did you ever see Nanet Carmichael?"

"Of course," Diana said eagerly. "The witch, you mean?"

"Fiddlesticks!" said the Doctor. "If every Scotswoman who was fey was called a witch there'd be an army of them."

"May I come with you?" Diana said impulsively. "Please let me," she added, as he hesitated before replying, "I am so bored here alone."

"Come away, then," he answered, and hastily fetching her coat she got into the motor-boat in which he made his rounds.

The water was calm enough today, and it seemed impossible to believe that, at any moment, it might rise dangerously. There was a grey sky with patches of brightness, but the peaks on the mainland were hidden under low clouds.

It was a short journey to Nanet's ramshackle hut on the beach, and as they neared her abode the doctor switched off the engine and propelled the boat the last few yards by hand.

"Seaweed does awful things with the propeller," he explained, and looking into the clear water beneath them, Diana saw a great forest of it, stretching out brown and red branches, like some lovely exotic shrub.

The Doctor sprang on to a broad, flat rock with the ease of one accustomed to such difficulties of landing. He dragged the boat as far as it would go, and assisted Diana to alight.

They had some way to walk over the green rocks, and several pools left behind by the tide to negotiate before they finally arrived at the dry shingle which led up to Nanet's cottage.

The Doctor knocked a rat-tat-tat on the rough board door, and a cracked, quavering voice bade him enter.

The hut was only a few feet square, the floor covered with rushes woven unskilfully into some semblance of a mat.

On a bed made from old boxes and pieces of driftwood Nanet was lying covered with a weird assortment of shawls and scraps of blanket, which she must have collected over a number of years. The only ventilation came from a cracked window, mostly covered with pieces of brown paper to keep out the draught.

Strangely enough, the hut was surprisingly clean but its comfortless state struck Diana as terribly pathetic. A huge packing-case served as a table and there was one broken kitchen chair which had probably been discarded from some more prosperous dwelling.

There was no warmth, for the brazier at which Nanet usually cooked and heated herself, arranged on a make-shift grate of roughly laid bricks, had not been lighted. Three cats, however, sat before it, in hopeful anticipation that it might warm them.

"I have brought you a visitor, Nanet," the Doctor said cheerily, beckoning Diana into the hut.

The old woman raised her head with difficulty, and regarded Diana. For a moment she seemed antagonistic to this uninvited guest, and then her toothless gums bared in an effort to smile, and she answered the Doctor in a quavering whisper which seemed to come with difficulty from her throat.

"Nanet says she remembers you," he said to Diana.

"Yes, I saw her once when I was riding this way. Tell her I am sorry she is so ill."

The Doctor repeated in Gaelic Diana's sympathy, but Nanet made no answer. She was staring fixedly at Diana, as she had done weeks before, when they had first met.

172

Then she pointed a bony finger at her and gabbled huskily for some moments, the doctor listening and nodding his head kindly, as though in agreement.

Diana could not understand a word, but there was no mistaking that Nanet was referring to her. She could hardly bear the suspense of waiting for the Doctor to translate, but when at last Nanet fell back weakly the Doctor took her pulse, speaking to her soothingly and kindly, without taking any further notice of Diana.

Finally, he handed her a bottle of medicine, produced as if miraculously from his pocket, and then, in a voice which told Diana he spoke cheeringly and hopefully, he said good-bye.

Nanet lay with closed eyes. She did not seem to hear the doctor's parting words or to notice Diana again, and they left, shutting the creaking door behind them, and clambered down to the beach.

"What did she say?" Diana said.

"She was in one of her prophetic moods," the Doctor answered. "No wonder the people around think her a witch. It is extraordinary the second-sight these simple people have. It is a compensation for lack of education, I suppose—though I am not sure that they miss the latter."

"But what did she say?" Diana repeated impatiently.

"She said you had stirred up trouble with a long spoon, and that you were wondering now how to quench the fires in your heart. She spoke in metaphors, of course, like they all do, but the gist of it, I imagine, was that you are your own worst enemy. Is that true?" he asked.

"I am afraid so," Diana answered. "I have been such a fool."

"So we all are, lassie, at times," he said kindly, "and we've got to learn by our own experience."

Diana nodded her agreement as she got back into the boat, and once again they started off along the coast.

"I am going to see a new godchild," he said. "Bless them, I am godfather to every child I bring into the world! They run well into their hundreds by this time, as you can imagine."

"But who christens them here?" Diana asked. "Do they go to the mainland?"

"Hoch, no!" he answered. "The minister comes round occasionally, but not often to Ronsa. The old Laird was against all form of religion, you know, and the people would rather have followed him than any parson's God. However, in point of fact, I generally christen them myself. The mothers are satisfied, and if it's faith that counts I don't suppose they will find it any more difficult to get to heaven than if it were done with all the correct ritual."

"Do you believe in God yourself?" Diana asked.

"Of course," he answered. "I could not have worked all these years without seeing and finding the wonder of His ways. There's nothing like living among simple people in a land which owes so much to Nature and so little to civilization to find that you must have help from something greater than yourself.

You can't telephone for assistance here if you are in trouble, like you can in a city. It takes sometimes days for anyone to find you if you are ill or starving or in dire distress. And it is then you need a Companion, and it is then you nearly always find Him."

"Perhaps you are right," Diana said. "I haven't thought much about it since I was a child. I used to be taken to long, dreary services by my grandmother, to hear at luncheon afterwards the parson roundly abused for the inadequacy of his sermon."

The Doctor laughed.

"Ay—I've not time for sermons, and little inclination to listen to them if I had. But as a panacea for every ill, a comfort whatever the disease—and most of us humans suffer from them, one way or another—I

174

find that God, and the belief in Him, is the only prescription which never fails."

He spoke with none of the pomposity, or in the solemn voice, which most people assume when discussing the Almighty. He chuckled over his similes, and spoke as naturally and lightly as if he were holding a commonplace conversation, but there was no doubting the sincerity of his own faith, and Diana felt that his was a logical creed, not merely a traditional one.

She was so interested in him that they had reached the end of the island before she realized it, and a moment later they were both clambering up the shallow, rough-hewn steps to the cliff's edge.

Surrounded by a small, neatly kept garden was a fisherman's hut. Nets were drying on every wooden fence, and a boat was dry-docked on tar-painted piles.

It was a three-roomed croft, and when they entered, Diana found it divided into equal halves, one side the kitchen and living-room, and the other side the bedroom, in which lay the mother and the baby which had been born the day before.

The Doctor accounted for Diana's presence, and she received a shy but sweet smile of welcome from the cheerful little woman sitting up in bed nursing her baby.

She seemed surprisingly well, but Diana learned afterwards she had had a very bad time, and, much against her will, had promised to stay quietly in bed until the Doctor's arrival today should allow her up.

Diana could hardly believe that anyone could rise so quickly after childbirth. How often had she visited her own friends in London, when they lay pale and exhausted four or five days after the event, being allowed five minutes' conversation only in the darkened, flower-scented room!

Yet tomorrow this woman would be about again as though nothing had happened—cleaning the house, getting her husband's meals, and at the same time tending and nursing her baby.

"Come and look at the bairn," the Doctor said to Diana as she stood a little embarrassed in the doorway, finding it difficult to visit people with whom she could not converse.

He drew aside a shawl and revealed a small red face, with tiny hands beating the air at being disturbed.

"It's Mary's first baby," he said, "and she's very pleased with it."

"Is it a boy or a girl?" Diana asked.

"A boy," he replied; "which makes her all the prouder. He will be a fisherman, like his father, and let's hope he will be as good a one!"

"Tell her I think he is very sweet," Diana said, and the Doctor translated her appreciation to Mary, who blushed and attempted to make Diana a little bow, though hampered by her pillows.

They stayed a few more moments, and then the doctor took Diana back to the Castle. All the way back she was thinking of that tiny face, and the mother who radiated such pride in its possession.

It would be strange to have a baby of one's own, she thought . . . and then a great desire filled her to have a son of Ian's in her arms.

Chapter 21

THE next day at the Castle passed very slowly for Diana. The Doctor had come first thing in the morning, before she was up, so she had not seen the cheery little man she already looked upon as a friend.

Luncheon with Sister Williams was a meal of uninspiring chit-chat, and an exchange of pleasantries which Diana found difficult to keep going until they had finished.

Sister Williams had an insatiable curiosity for the doings of young Society; but Diana found it increasingly hard to answer her questions; she was evidently, Diana gathered, expecting to be regaled with wild stories of orgies.

She was disappointed that Diana's accounts were so dull. Cocktail-parties were, in her imagination, so gay a dissipation that Diana found it impossible to convey to her how extremely boring and innocuous they invariably were.

Sister Williams expected every well-known man to be violently in love, either with a notorious actress or a film star, and every Society beauty to be pursued by an endless attendance of fascinating young men.

If only it were true, Diana thought wearily—and wearily she disclaimed any knowledge of whom the Prince of Wales was to marry, or if Evelyn Laye was affianced to a Duke. . . .

"Well, I have heard . . ." Sister Williams would begin, and never before had Diana received such intimate information of the morals of her friends and acquaintances, or of their internal complaints.

Sister Williams had a friend who had nursed Lady So-and-so, or a friend of that friend had massaged Lord This-or-that after his hunting-accident, and they had told her, or had told the friend who told her, of such goings-on and such intrigues, that finally Diana remained quite unsurprised when informed that her most Puritan-minded and strait-laced aunt was having an affair with her own chauffeur.

Yet, though she was impatient of all this, she could not help understanding that Sister Williams and her friends had little else to liven their dull lives.

It was case after case, each requiring their utmost attention and care, and if, while they gave their bodies

177

in endless service, their minds wandered into fantastic fields, one could not blame them for enjoying other people's enjoyment, for they had so little in their own lives.

There was no doubt that Sister Williams was a singularly efficient nurse, utterly unselfish, unceasingly attentive to her patient, and very conscientious. Sister McLeod was the same.

After a long night on her feet, hardly snatching a moment's rest from Ian's bedside, she would run smilingly downstairs for a quick breakfast before retiring to bed, and Diana, even while they irritated her, gave wholehearted admiration to the two women.

Sister Williams was fair, and had a nice face, her looks only being spoilt by irregular teeth, slightly prominent. This, however, did not prevent her receiving all sorts of strange attentions from her patients.

Diana was astounded that men could be so peculiarly minded—unless Sister Williams had been singularly fortunate in her patients. And the Doctors!

"You wouldn't believe, Lady Diana," she said solemnly, so obviously enjoying her confidences that Diana hadn't the heart to stop her—"you would never imagine what a time we have sometimes in hospital. I remember one day, soon after I joined as a probationer, I was scrubbing the passage outside the operating-theatre, when one of the Doctors—of course he was young, but old enough to know better—called me into the theatre.

He was alone there, and—well, I hardly like to tell you what he suggested . . . enough, anyway, for me to feel ashamed of the whole profession—as I told him. He apologized when I had finished, and I was only eighteen, and a probationer too—but of course I was in the right and he knew it."

"Of course," Diana murmured.

"I'm not saying they are all like that—by no means," continued Sister Williams. "There's Dr. Simpson, for

178

instance. He is adored by everyone—some of the girls are quite stupid about it, feel faint when he speaks to them and such-like, but he never forgets his position, that's what I admire. Of course, he has his favourite nurses, who are used to his ways"—

Sister Williams looked self-conscious—

"And very considerate of them he is too, but nothing more, mind you. As I once said to Sister McLeod: 'If that man were alone with a lady on a desert island, he'd treat her like a lady and behave like a gentleman' —which is more than you can say of most men these days."

"Is it?" Diana said, seeing a comment was expected of her.

"My dear Lady Diana, you're only a child—if you'll excuse me saying so—but you'll find, as I have, there are few men you can trust in the world, especially if you have . . . well—please forgive the word!—'It' . . . or should I say 'sex appeal'? . . . Believe me—I know!"

And Sister Williams again looked roguishly self-conscious.

"And does Sister McLeod have trouble of that sort?" Diana could not resist inquiring.

"Well, between ourselves," answered Sister Williams, dropping her voice to a piercing whisper, although Sister McLeod was asleep upstairs, "just confidentially, because I don't think Sister would like me to tell you, she has a broken heart."

"No!" ejaculated Diana, for it was the last thing she expected Sister McLeod's fat cheerfulness to hide.

"It's a very sad story," Sister Williams said, shaking her head—"quite pathetic, in fact. Of course, I think she was misguided, as I told her myself, one is often too hasty—but still, I must start from the beginning— only of course you promise that you will never let her guess that you know?"

"Of course not," Diana assured her.

"Well, it was a long time ago—Sister must have

179

been about twenty-eight. She was quite thin then, and really pretty at times, when she took the trouble. She was sent to a case in Edinburgh—one of our own doctors was operating, so naturally he asked for two of us. I couldn't go with her, because I was already engaged, but another nurse accompanied her.

"Sister McLeod told me that, when she saw the patient, she knew it was going to be a stiff job. His name was Mr. Munro. Not only was his operation to be a severe abdominal one, but he was in a terrible state of exhausted nerves, from months of pain. From the moment he saw Sister, he took a fancy to her, and soon he refused to let the other nurse come near him, and they had to humour him, for he was so ill.

"Sister McLeod snatched her sleep when she could, she was up night and day for nearly three weeks; then he turned the corner, and she practically collapsed herself. But still she didn't leave. Mr. Munro wouldn't hear of that, and the Doctors gave in to him; patients always count before nurses.

"Anyway, that was when the trouble began—Sister McLeod was an orphan, few people had made a fuss of her in her life, none had clung to her.

"She felt tender towards his helplessness, having literally snatched him away from death—and you know they always say pity is akin to love. Anyway, she fell more and more for him, and dreaded the moment when she would have to go.

"As he got better he began to notice things, and it was not long before it had got to good-morning and good-night kisses—and at other times, I dare say, when they were alone.

"Then one day, he said, 'I shall miss you, Ethel, when you've gone'—they'd got to Christian names by this time—and she sort of choked, and he said, 'I love you, and I think you love me, but I expect you know I'm married.'

180

"She didn't—no one had ever hinted at such a thing, and it was a terrible shock. Sister McLeod is a Presbyterian, and she would never have let herself have fancies about a married man.

"But it was too late then, she was head over heels in love with him, and things weren't much better when he told her he was separated from his wife, who hated the sight of him, and that they never met.

"Of course, he wanted Sister to live with him, offered to go anywhere in the world with her, but she packed her box and departed that very day. He wrote once or twice, but she returned his letters. . . . Between ourselves, I think she's sorry now. She never had another chance—wouldn't have cared for it if she had.

"She was right, of course, yet sometimes I think she may have missed a lot of happiness. He loved her in the right way, and she mightn't have regretted it . . . still, one never knows, does one?"

"Poor Sister McLeod!" Diana spoke softly.

"That's just what I feel, Lady Diana—yet she seems happy enough now. . . . Dear, dear, how I do run on —and it's time for my patient to be awake."

Sister Williams bustled away.

After the day of her arrival, Diana had not seen Jean. Sister McLeod had evidently coped very successfully with the situation, and if Jean called to inquire she was not told of her arrival.

Diana spent the rest of the day trying to read, but failing dismally. She could not even persuade herself into going for a walk, and in spite of the Doctor's orders she refused to ride any of Ian's horses. She somehow felt that, without his permission, she could not. The memory of Starlight prevented her.

She moved disconsolately about the Castle, touching this and that, striving to be amused by a book of photographs, or any of the strange curiosities lying about, but after a moment she would put them down

181

and wander on to the next object to attract her attention.

Everywhere, she found, she was haunted by the thought of Ian's presence; sometimes she would glance up quickly, half expecting to see him stride into the room.

The Castle was so redolent of him, and every nook and corner brought a fresh stab of memory to torture her with the thought of the wasted hours she had spent sulking, when she might have been so happy.

The sitting-room where he had lifted her in his arms to carry her to bed, the table over which they had faced each other silently or in discordance, the sofa where she had always rested in the evenings, the huge chair opposite, where he had sat, the dogs at his feet.

The dogs, indeed, were a great consolation to her now, yet, like herself, they wanted Ian. They suffered her caresses, but at the slightest sound they would listen, alert for their master to come to them.

They knew he was ill, for they would sit for hours outside his door waiting, yet making no attempt to enter after the first day, when the room had been forbidden them.

How devoted Ian was to his animals! Diana remembered how one day they had returned from a ride to find that his Great Dane, Rollo, had cut his paw in their absence on a piece of glass. The dog was in pain and bleeding freely.

He would not allow any one of the servants to approach him, growling ferociously at their attempts to dress the wound, showing his teeth in a snarl which made them unwilling to try.

Yet from the moment of Ian's entrance he lay still and submitted to his master bandaging his foot, even allowing him to bathe it in a disinfectant which must have stung. He whined a little and moved restlessly, but otherwise was as quiet as a sleeping child.

Diana had marvelled at the neat skill with which Ian bandaged, and then she remembered how often in his explorations he must have had to act as Doctor and nurse, not only to himself but to his companions.

He had been kind and gentle to her, the night before she left. He had known that her nerves were near breaking-point, had looked after her as tenderly as though he had been her mother. He had taken her wet shoes from her cold feet, and rubbed them until the circulation returned.

When she was in bed, he had entered the room, but with no other intention than seeing that she was all right and of putting another log on the fire.

How she wished now she had been ill after her failure to escape! Why could not she have had a bad cold, anything which would have kept her in bed, and prevented Jean approaching her? If only she were ill now, instead of Ian! She even fancied she would enjoy the pain.

The night brought her fitful dreams. Once she had a nightmare that she herself was drowning, but that she was alone in a vast expanse of water, with no one to save her.

Into the dream came Jean, sweeping past her in a motor-boat, her angry, revengeful face ignoring her plight, and though Diana called for help, she passed her by, and again she was alone.

She woke to find her hands and forehead wet with sweat, and it took her a long time before she again fell into a drowsy slumber. This time she dreamed she was in Ian's arms, and she awoke to hear her own voice saying.

"I love you! Don't you understand!—I love you!"

Morning found her with a splitting headache, and dark lines beneath her eyes. The Doctor arrived at noon, and instantly threatened a tonic if she did not look better next day, but when he came downstairs from his visit to Ian, before she could ask the inevitable question of how the patient was, he said:

"I have thought of a better medicine for you. If you wish it, you shall see the invalid for just two minutes."

The colour rushed to Diana's cheeks, and with a thudding heart she followed him upstairs.

"We have not told him you are here," said the Doctor. "We thought, maybe, he might worry at your being alone. I don't say I am right, mind you, to surprise him like this, but still, I will take the risk, or I shall have two patients on my hands instead of one."

In her happy anticipation, Diana did not answer him. Sister Williams turned the door-handle noiselessly, and they entered the room.

The blinds were half-drawn, but the room was not dark. Ian was lying on his bed with closed eyes. He looked so pale that Diana's heart contracted at the sight. His left arm was in a sling, and there was a bandage across his forehead.

Timidly she drew nearer the bed. What would he say when he saw her? Even the Doctor did not know of their parting. Otherwise she guessed he would not have allowed her in. She was frightened, even terrified, of upsetting Ian, and yet she was too weak to refuse to see him.

It seemed as though she had waited centuries for this moment, not two days. The Doctor was in front of her, and he spoke very gently.

"I have a visitor for you, Ian my boy."

"For God's sake, don't admit condolences," Ian said, his voice weak and faint, as if it came from his lips with an effort, but he strove to smile faintly at his own humour.

"Well, I should hardly call this a condolence," the Doctor answered; "and she has been waiting patiently enough for the privilege of seeing you."

Slowly Ian opened his eyes until they rested on

Diana. He gave a little start, and his whole body seemed to stiffen.

"You!" he said faintly.

The Doctor had moved aside at his last remark to let Diana approach nearer. Tactfully, he had walked away towards the dressing-table, seemingly finding interest in the temperature-chart which was standing propped against the looking-glass.

"Why are you here?" Ian said, and Diana for a moment could not speak. The sight of him had unnerved her, more even than she had expected.

He looked so ill, so unlike his strong self. She felt as though she were choking. She clasped her hands together in an effort to control the emotions which seemed likely to overcome her.

"I came back——" she faltered at last.

"You are to go away," Ian interrupted. "Do you hear me? You are to go away at once."

His voice rose with the intensity he put into the words, and the Doctor, at the sound, hurried across the room.

"Hush!" he said, taking his pulse. "You mustn't get excited."

"She's to go away," Ian repeated, "do you hear? She's to go home—away from here."

"Hush—hush!"

Ian was obviously upset. He was trying to raise his head from the pillow. Diana stood as if turned to stone, then suddenly something seemed to snap inside her, and she could not prevent the tears welling into her eyes and blinding her.

She rushed from the room, almost knocking over Sister Williams, who was in the doorway, alarmed at the sound of Ian's voice.

And as she went, unseeingly, down the long corridor to her room, she heard in the distance the voice she loved crying wildly:

"She must go away . . . she is to go at once!"

Chapter 22

IT was the Doctor who made all arrangements for Diana's departure next day. She was so upset that she felt quite incapable of planning anything for herself.

She did not want to leave the Castle, but could not insist on staying in face of Ian's protestations against her, which were known not only to the Doctor but to both the nurses.

Up to the last moment, she hoped that he would ask for her, and that once alone with him she could persuade him to let her wait for his recovery.

When the Doctor finally came to fetch her, taking her in his motor-boat to Torvish, she said:

"I don't want to go—I hate going. Can't you ask Ian——?"

"I have," he interrupted, and she knew that her last hope had gone.

"Good-bye," she said, with a pathetic little smile, as the train came rumbling into the station, "and thank you for being so kind to me."

"God keep ye, lassie," he answered, holding her hand in both of his, "and remember that mistakes can be rectified sooner or later, but it requires patience and grit."

"I'll remember," Diana promised, and on an impulse kissed him.

"There, there, lassie!" he said, helping her into the carriage, and he waved until the train carried her out of sight.

Even when it had finally disappeared he still stood for a while, staring down the empty line, in deep thought; then he walked slowly away.

Diana's last glimpse of the Castle made her feel as if she had left part of herself behind in its keeping. Even if Ian forgot her, if she never returned to Ronsa, she knew she would never again be the same person who landed there in that strange airplane elopement not quite a month ago.

She had no idea how she was going to spend the next four weeks before her parents returned from America. She was entirely on her own, and there was nothing to stop her going wherever she wished. Yet, somehow, this freedom held little enchantment for her.

She felt too tired and utterly weary of life to contemplate being entertained by any of her gay friends, and when she had mentally reviewed the more sober ones, she felt she could not bear the well-meaning attentions they would feel bound to pour out upon her at the least hint that she desired peace and rest.

She knew her reputation for gaiety would not allow them to put any other application on such a desire but that of an unfortunate love-affair.

However, she arrived at Grosvenor Square to find things decided for her. She was met by the news that Ellen was seriously ill. She had caught a chill, which had developed into rheumatic fever.

Being very old, and having been ailing for years, Ellen had no strength left to combat an illness, and the Doctor told Diana quite frankly there was no hope of saving her life.

Nothing could have upset Diana so much as the thought of losing Ellen, and, like most of us do, she only realized now, when it was too late, how little return she had given for Ellen's twenty-five years of selfless devotion to herself.

Diana could not remember a time or even a moment in her life when Ellen had not been there to serve her, whatever her necessity.

She remembered how she had adored her when a child. Lady Stanlier, like most fashionable mothers, visited the nursery perhaps twice a day, but Ellen was always there, ready first to guide her faltering steps, later to guide and mould her character as best she might.

It would have been better, perhaps, if she had not loved Diana so intensely. It was inevitable that she should spoil her, but Ellen was of a temperament entirely and absolutely maternal—she would have made a perfect mother, had she accepted the opportunities she received of marriage.

But any inclinations she may have had for such a position were forgotten after she came to Diana. The child clung to her, and Ellen relinquished entirely any private life she might have had before.

Lady Stanlier was even faintly jealous of Ellen, knowing that the nurse stood higher in the affections of the child than the mother. Yet Ellen was so eminently trustworthy that she could not help finding it a blessing to know that her daughter was in such safe keeping.

And now Ellen was lying frail and wasted, no longer able to serve, but still in her dying, as in her living, thinking only of Diana.

The Doctors had seen that her last hours were to be easy, untouched by pain, and Diana was allowed to go to her as soon as she arrived. There were tears in her eyes as she bent over the old woman.

"You're unhappy, dearie," Ellen whispered, her voice very weak.

"I can't bear you to be ill, Ellen," Diana answered.

Ellen looked at her with eyes wise from a long knowledge of her feelings.

"It is not only me," she said; "there's something else."

Diana could not lie—what was more, she knew it

was useless. If no one else had, Ellen had always received and known the truth from and of her.

"There is, Ellen," she confessed, "but don't bother about it, darling."

"Tell me—who is it?" Ellen asked.

"I am not going to worry you now," she said, but Ellen was not to be dissuaded.

"I haven't got much longer," she said, "and I want to know before I die. . . . There, there, dearie," she added, as Diana gave a sudden sob, "it is no use worrying. We've all got to give up some time, and I am happy to go."

Diana controlled her sobs with difficulty. She knew it would upset Ellen if she broke down completely.

"Who is it?" Ellen asked again, and Diana, remembering the nurse's instructions—"you may talk to her, but she must not try to talk too much to you"—thought it best to prevaricate no longer.

"It is Ian Carstairs," she said, the mere fact of saying his name making her heart ache.

"Do you love him, dearie?"

Ellen looked at her, and knew the answer before Diana nodded in reply.

"He is the only one of them all that's worthy of you," she said. "It will come right, dearie—don't worry. He loves you . . . I knew it when I first saw him, and Ellen is not easy to deceive. He is worthy of you," she repeated in a whisper, and closed her eyes, as if the effort of talking was too much.

For a long time she lay like that, Diana sitting beside her; then she opened her eyes again.

"My Diana!" she said, as if talking to herself. . . . "He is a fine man . . . I would have liked dearly to have seen their children."

She gave a little sigh, and seemed asleep. There was a smile on her face the whole long afternoon that Diana sat beside her in the darkened room.

The nurse tried to take her place, but Diana refused.

She knew Ellen had little more time with her, and she would not forgo a moment of it.

How many hours, she wondered, if they were totalled up, could Ellen have spent watching over her cradle, her cot, and, when she was older, she knew that a night seldom passed without Ellen rousing herself two or three times to tiptoe into her room to see if she were all right.

In later years, when Ellen had become an invalid, it had been agony for her not to see to Diana's comfort the last thing at night.

In her room at the top of the house she would question the housemaids until they were almost frantic, wanting to know exactly if the fire was right, the window open just so much, the clothes arranged, the drink by Diana's bed.

Then she would lie awake, if Diana were out, listening for the sound of her returning—a car driving up, voices outside, the slam of the front door, and her footsteps coming upstairs.

It was useless to resent her anxiety, and utterly useless to try to persuade her not to worry. Often, Diana now thought bitterly, she had condemned her as tiresome. How deeply she would miss that tiresomeness now!

She would have told Ellen the whole story of Ian sooner or later—that was inevitable, for Ellen knew everything about Diana, the good, the bad, the kind, the unkind, the nice, and the horrible. All the things she did, practically all she thought, sooner or later were confessed to Ellen.

She listened sympathetically, yet striving to help and advise her as best she could.

Diana felt she would have liked Ellen to have heard her story of Ronsa. To no one else could she dare make the slightest mention, even of Ian himself—but Ellen would have helped her, would have straightened the chaos of her mind and feelings, have unknotted the skein which emotion had tangled. But now she would never know, and Diana was utterly alone.

It was dusk before the old woman roused herself again. She had a slight palpitation, and the nurse was hurriedly summoned to her side.

They raised her a little on her pillows, and she opened her eyes, seeking, of course, the sight of Diana.

"My baby!" she said affectionately.

Then it seemed as though her memory went far, far into the past, for she said, very gently, as though to a sleepy child:

"Good night, darling, and God bless you."

She gave a little sigh, as if her life was completed, and she was dead.

The days that followed, and the funeral, were a nightmare of loss and misery. Diana endured as if in a dream.

She could not realize, could not really believe, that Ellen was no longer with them, and it was only when the little room, where she had lived her last years, was closed and empty that Diana knew how terribly she was going to suffer without her.

Lord Stanlier's brother came from the country to make arrangements for the burial, and, Diana's looks horrifying him, he sent her away to the sea.

"The cure for most complaints," Diana thought miserably, "but mine are mental, and I doubt if the change will do me good."

However, she was too weary to protest much, and in spite of her unhappiness the sea air and rest did help her to gain her balance.

She went to Devonshire, to her uncle's house; but luckily no one was there but the servants, and she spent the warm days lying on the beach in her bathing-dress, with as companions only the gulls and the cormorants, which looked at her from the cliffs.

It was a lovely place. The house was built at the mouth of a small river where it widened into the sea, causing a sand bar over which the waves broke on the calmest day. Stone steps were cut down the red cliffs, and the sea, blue as the Mediterranean in the sunshine, lapped the golden sands.

There was no village, only a row of thatched fishermen's cottages, and a tiny "pub", where the draught cider was delicious.

Diana would go there sometimes at noon, after bathing, and sit in the bar on a rough oak bench, a huge pewter mug in her hand.

Tom Broom, who kept the "Ancient Mariner", was a "charatcer". A huge man, of enormous physique, he had once been a boxing fisherman, known and feared for his brutality, but marriage had softened and fattened him.

He was now the gentlest person imaginable, and devoted to his children, who obviously adored him.

When Diana first met the woman who had worked this miracle, she nearly laughed, for Mrs. Broom was the smallest normal woman she had ever seen. A few inches shorter, and she would have been a dwarf, but she was perfectly proportioned, and must have been exceedingly attractive in her youth, and it was quite understandable that Tom had been attracted by her.

He could have broken her between his thumb and forefinger, and, as she hardly reached to his elbow walking together they were the most ludicrous pair imaginable. But Tom was terrified of her.

She commanded—he obeyed. If he argued, or was slow, she would flash out at him like some impertinent puppy yapping at a mastiff, and Tom would shamefacedly apologize and do her will.

Their two boys, luckily, had taken after their father. They were broad-shouldered and big-boned, and promised to grow into fine men.

Their mother was inordinately proud of them, but Tom's fancy was for his daughter—a tiny little creature, who, at five years old, could still sleep in a cot and who danced gaily and blithely about the house like a captured fairy.

"She's lovely, Tom," Diana told him, as blue eyes peeped shyly at her through a mist of curly, ash-blonde hair. "You'll have to keep the men off with a stick in a year or two!"

Tom laughed, a great, braw laugh which did one good to hear.

"But her mother'll see to that," he said. "The plans she has for 'em children would cost the earth, and bankrupt us. Billie is for the Navy, Roland for the Merchant Service, and Jennie—now, what do you think she wants o' Jennie?"

"I can't guess," Diana answered. "Tell me."

"She's to go to a boarding-school, like a lady," Tom said impressively. "Did you ever?"

"I think Mrs. Broom is very wise," Diana answered.

"She be that," Tom agreed, "and ambitious—you wouldn't believe the ambition that woman has. At one time, it was for me to be on the County Council—me!"

His laughter again echoed through the rafters.

"Can ye see me, all dolled up, to sit with 'em serious bodies?"

At that moment, curious as to the cause of her husband's merriment, Mrs. Broom put her head through the hatch.

"Oh, good day to you, milady," she said hastily, when she saw Diana, checking the words of rebuke she had ready for Tom.

"I was hearing about your family," Diana told her, smiling. "So Jennie is to go to a boarding-school?"

"Not for some years, milady—it's the boys who will leave us first." A shadow crossed her face. "I'd dearly like to show you their new photo."

"Oh, do," Diana urged her, and Mrs. Broom's head disappeared.

A moment later she entered through the doorway, holding delicately a photograph of the two boys. Stiffly posed against a studio stile, their expressions set and serious, and unbelievably clean and tidy.

Diana could hardly recognize the two jolly children she could see playing outside, their hair tousled, their faces as grubby as their fishermen's jerseys, barefooted, and handsome enough, as they were, to be worthy of an artist's brush.

But to Mrs. Broom there was no comparison.

"They look fine, don't they?" she said proudly, referring to the photograph. "But, my! They won't keep like that. Look at the young varmints now!"

"They are so happy and healthy! I shouldn't worry about them," Diana replied.

"Just what Oi say," bellowed Tom. "Never a day's illness, that's better than all the smart clothes—eh, Mother?"

Mrs. Broom smiled, but only faintly. It was obvious that one of her ambitions was to possess model children of the Little Lord Fauntleroy type. She hurried to the street door.

"Billie! Roland!" she called. "Come here at once. Go and wash y'selves, you dirty boys! I can't think how you get so filthy—it's wash, wash, wash for me all day at y'clothes. I'm ashamed of you both—go along in."

Sheepishly the boys obeyed.

"She's a fine woman," Tom said, as his wife disappeared into the back of the house after them, still scolding. "She'll work herself to the bone for 'em children. A bit faddy-like, but they don't mind really, bless 'em. They know she'd do aught she could for them at any time, and that's what counts, ain't it? Better be loved anyhow than not loved at all, says Oi."

"You are quite right," Diana agreed.

When she felt physically better, she took stock of herself, and she knew that whatever had happened to her life, however much she missed Ellen, however greatly she wanted Ian, she could not and must not crumple under her failure to attain her desires.

Her life must go on, even if she were maimed, as it seemed to her that she was. It was as though only part of her was in being—the other half, she felt, was divided between Ronsa and the little grave in Kensal Green where Ellen lay.

But one could not just lie down and cease to exist—and Diana, who had always despised weakness, realized that her weakness now was making her despicable to herself.

"Where is my pride?" she asked. "Where is the courage I always believed I had?"

Yet somehow she understood that these things, which she had always regarded as part of her, when faced with reality, were not so sustaining as she had imagined.

It was easy to risk one's life riding or motoring, or even in other pleasurable pursuits with an element of danger, but it was difficult to face without flinching the fact that you could not attain the only things which made your life worth while.

It had been easy to be proud, when one believed in one's own omnipotence, but difficult when one had fallen below one's own standards.

But however much Diana belittled herself to herself, her courage and pride were really there. Tried by the fire of suffering, they rose true and flawless to face the future.

Chapter 23

DIANA returned to London a few days before her parents disembarked at Southampton, and she took up again the threads of her social life.

Her friends were gradually drifting home from the Riviera, from Scotland, and from the many places all the world over where they had sought holiday.

Most of them sensed a change in Diana, even though they could not account for or explain it.

She was none the less beautiful, but there was a softness about her face and a depth of character in her expression which had not been there before, and her manner and behaviour were less defiant, less overbearingly strident.

She was more tolerant, less impatient when she was unable to have her own way; and though all these things were not at first apparent to her acquaintances, they gradually began to notice them, and they cared for her with a deeper liking than the mere superficial affection they had given to her brilliance before.

Lady Stanlier was puzzled by her daughter. She could not have believed that Ellen's death could have wrought such a change.

Diana was often at home these days, and her parents, on their return, saw more of her in the space of seven days than, ordinarily, they would have had the opportunity of enjoying in as many months.

With the humbleness of modern parents confronted

with modern youth, they had not expected Diana to find any amusement in their company.

They were only too conscious that they were boring to most young people, and that the opinions they had gathered through years of life, and the experience of those years, were considered utterly valueless beside the sophisticated utterances of some immature youth.

Diana had been no exception to the general rule. She had liked her parents well enough; kissed them perfunctorily on meeting, but dismissed them as "slow, and a little tiresome, poor dears".

When she actually sought their society, they were at first half suspicious, and so ingenuously surprised that an outsider would have found the situation amusing, if a little pathetic.

"Your bank account overdrawn?" her father asked her, when Diana, for the first time since she had grown up, offered to accompany him on a round of golf.

"No," Diana answered. "Why?"

And he, bewildered at her attention, and inwardly rather flattered, gave up the attempt to probe this sudden filial agreeableness.

"But, darling, you will be so bored," Lady Stanlier protested, when Diana announced her intention of accompanying her to one of the many charity shows which took up so much of her time.

"Of course, I am delighted if you want to come," she added quickly, "but you know how dull you generally find these entertainments."

"I'd like it, Mummy—I really would," Diana answered, and Lady Stanlier, quite fluttered with the unusualness of the occasion, spent the afternoon introducing Diana to her many acquaintances, showing off her beautiful daughter as proudly as a hen a newly hatched chick.

There was no news for Diana from the North. Week after week the hope died slowly that perhaps she would hear from Ian; and when finally she did not, she told herself she must be sensible and forget.

But words or resolutions were useless against the unreasonableness of her whole self, which ached with never-ceasing want of him.

In October she was laid up with a slight chill, nothing serious, but enough to keep her indoors for two weeks, which seemed unbearably long.

Among her letters one morning was one in a round, precise handwriting which she did not recognize.

When she opened it, she turned immediately to the signature, and found it signed "Florence Williams". There were many sheets, closely written, and headed with an address in Lossiemouth.

Dear Lady Diana (she read),

I have been meaning to write to you ever since I left Ronsa, but have been so busy.

As soon as Mr. Carstairs was well enough to be left, Sister McLeod and myself were sent straight off to a patient in Caithness, an old lady who had broken her leg. She was eighty-two—think of it! —and mentally not a bit the worse for her accident.

From there I came here, and had a pretty difficult time for the first week, as my patient—a retired colonel—had a temperature of over 104° the whole time. However, he is at last convalescent, and I can find time to take up my pen.

After you left, Mr. Carstairs had a slight relapse, but nothing very serious. We had no visitors until a week before Sister McLeod and myself were leaving, and then that Miss Ross got permission from the doctor to see him. I personally thought it most unwise, knowing how she had behaved to you, but still you know what Doctors are, and it was no use us interfering.

So she went to see him, and there was evidently

a tremendous to-do, though we never heard exactly what had happened.

Anyway, she came downstairs in tears, and Mr. Carstairs seemed most upset the whole evening, quite glum, and not a bit like his usual self.

I told the doctor, of course, and he didn't say anything, but, to our surprise, within a few days Margaret told us that he—the Doctor—had found Miss Ross a position on the mainland, as secretary to a hospital some way up the coast. She never came to the Castle to say good-bye or anything, but I happened to be out for a walk, and saw her leaving, and I couldn't help thinking it was a good riddance, anyway.

I am just dreading going back to hospital, for I hear that dear Dr. Simpson has left, and goodness knows what sort of man we shall get in his place. I hate changes—I always find that "new brooms" have no idea who really know their work and who don't.

I often think of you, and look for your name in the papers. I expect you are having a gay time. Anyway, I sincerely trust that one day we will meet again. I often think of our little chats together.

> *Yours very sincerely,*
> *Florence Williams.*

Diana read again the description of Jean's departure. So the serpent had left Eden, she thought—but, even so, the role of Eve was no longer required of her.

She wondered for a long time what could really have happened between Ian and Jean. She had, of course, a shrewd suspicion, but even so her mind was too glutted with her own emotions for her to be certain of anything where Ian was concerned.

While she was still thinking, the telephone beside

her rang sharply, and it was Rosemary who answered her "Hullo!"

"Darling," Rosemary said breathlessly, "I must see you—it is terribly important. Can I come round at once?"

"Of course," Diana said. "I am alone—come straight up to my room."

"I shall be five minutes," Rosemary replied.

Diana wondered what was wrong. Rosemary and Lord Leadhold had returned from the South of France together, so she could not believe there was any trouble in that quarter. However, well within the five minutes she had promised, Rosemary arrived.

She was looking pale, rather dishevelled, and quite unlike her usual self. She kissed Diana effusively, and sank on to a chair, evidently determined not to waste a moment before she commenced her story.

"What is it, Rosemary dear?" Diana asked.

"I could never have believed it possible," Rosemary burst out. "Never! If I'd even dreamt of such a thing. I should never have gone away—and now to return to find this! Though why it should happen is beyond my comprehension. It is such a shock, I hardly know how to tell anyone—even you, Diana!"

She paused for breath.

"Give me a cigarette," she said.

Diana handed her one from the enamelled box beside her bed, and Rosemary lit it.

"Do start at the beginning," Diana said. "Tell me quickly—what is the matter?"

"It's Henry," Rosemary said.

"Henry!" Diana echoed.

He was the last person she expected to be responsible for Rosemary's agitation.

"I thought he was odd when I returned," Rosemary continued—"different, with a rather self-conscious manner, as though he'd been up to mischief. At first I took no notice—I thought perhaps he wasn't feeling well, had caught a cold, or that the constituency was bothering him. And then Vera told me she had seen him once or twice, and teased me about some attractive brunette he had been with.

"Of course, I didn't listen—you know how devoted Henry is to me, and how there has never been another woman in his life. Then, to make a long story short, I became a tiny bit worried, only to have my worst suspicions realized when I discovered a letter. The most terrible letter darling; abusing me and suggesting all sorts of things to Henry!

"Apparently the woman is a Mrs. Peachey—Ruby Peachey, no one we know, of course—in fact, hardly a lady. I would not have minded so much if she had been. And, my dear, they had been away together for several week-ends while I was in the South of France!

"I can hardly believe it now—Henry of all people! Even with the evidence before my own eyes, I thought it must be a lie. But when I tackled him, he confessed everything. He is in love with her, if you please, and wants to marry her!"

Diana was quite as astonished as Rosemary could have wished, but she could not help, in spite of feeling sorry for her friend's distress, thinking that perhaps poor Henry was rather justified.

Granted he had behaved extremely stupidly, even dishonourably, about Rosemary's affair with Lord Leadhold, making excuses and even accepting every advantage his wife could obtain for him. But there was no denying Rosemary had neglected him more and more, and had gone to the South of France for two months, without a thought for his entertainment or well-being while she was away.

"How strange women are," Diana reflected. Rosemary didn't really want Henry herself, she had no love for him, and very little affection, but she could not bear another woman to have him, or for his interests to centre away from herself.

But Rosemary was obviously very distressed, and she did her best to soothe and console her.

"But I don't want to divorce Henry," she kept saying "I like being married to him, and after all, we get along very well on the whole. He will be miserable with this woman—of course he will. No one has ever understood him as well as I have. Think of what I have put up with—his poverty, his inability to push himself, his laziness and lack of initiative—and now, just when he is on the threshold of a successful political career, he wants to chuck it all for some common woman he has picked up God knows where!"

"What does Leadhold say about it?" Diana asked.

"The old boy is furious," Rosemary replied. "He can't marry me, even if I am free. His wife is only forty-five, and she'll go on living for ever, and a man in his position can't have a scandal. It was so easy with Henry as a background—no one could say anything about our friendship as long as my husband approved. Now things are going to be impossibly complicated. It is not only unkind of Henry, it is extraordinarily inconsiderate."

She rose to her feet and adjusted her hat in the glass.

"I don't know yet what I am going to do, and I am most terribly upset," she said. "I had to tell you, darling, because I knew you would sympathize. I think Henry has behaved like a cad, and I have told him so. . . .

"Are you better?" she asked casually, just as she got to the door, suddenly remembering that Diana had been ill, but she hardly listened to Diana's answer, speeding away so engrossed in her own troubles that she had no time for other people's.

She had hardly gone, when Lady Stanlier came upstairs, her arms filled with an enormous bunch of red and white carnations.

"They are from Ronald, darling," she said, "and he is waiting downstairs—Rosemary has borrowed his
202

car. He says he would simply love to see you for a moment, but will quite understand if you don't want to."

"Of course!" Diana said. "I'd like to see him."

Ronald, looking very handsome and sunburnt, a little embarrassed, but very anxious to be pleasant, shook her by the hand, then sat down beside the bed.

"I am terribly sorry you have been ill," he said, and Diana smiled at him.

"I am much better now," she answered, "and I think it's very sweet of you to bring me all those lovely flowers."

"I only got back last night," he replied, "and as soon as I heard, came rushing round."

"You're a dear," she thanked him.

"You don't mind seeing me again, do you?" Ronald questioned.

"Of course not," Diana said. "You know we've always been friends, Ronald, and we've had a great deal of fun together. It was all my fault that"—she hesitated—"there was anything else. Have you forgiven me now?"

"Look here, Diana"—Ronald bent forward earnestly—"I don't want to talk about things if you would rather not. I know you and most people think I am a complete fool, and I quite realize I am not good enough or clever enough for you. But I'd like frightfully to help you if I could. You won't mind my saying something?"

"No," Diana answered.

"Well, after you'd gone," Ronald said, "I puzzled my brains for a long time to think what could have upset things like that. And then I found the paper you had been reading—you had taken it up to your room, do you remember?—the night of the dance, I mean—and . . . well, I sort of guessed it was something to do with Carstairs. If I am wrong, forgive me."

"You're quite right," Diana said quietly, and suddenly something made her add: "I love him, Ronald."

"I thought very likely that you did," Ronald replied gravely. "But doesn't that make everything all right?"

Diana shook her head.

"No," she answered. "I can't tell anyone about it—not even you, Ronald. He did care for me once, but now—and it's all my fault—he hates me."

"Hates you!" Ronald echoed in surprise. "Why, the man must——"

But Diana held up her hand.

"No, please, Ronald—don't! You don't understand. It honestly isn't his fault. It's absolutely and entirely mine. I have behaved—well, shall we say, like a b—— fool?—and now it's too late."

There was a little silence between them, and then Ronald put out his hand and took hers.

"Look here, Diana darling," he said, "you know how I feel for you, and all that. It's rotten luck, and I'd do anything in the world to make things come right for your happiness. I love you, and I think I always shall, but I 'ain't got no 'opes', as the coster said. But if you want someone to amble around with, however you're feeling, call on me, won't you?"

"Ronald . . ." Diana said, and just for a moment she could not go on.

There were tears in her eyes at his sweetness. He was being so awfully kind—and kindness these days made her feel rather choky, somehow.

"Now don't let us talk any more about it," Ronald said with his usual brightness. "Cheer up, solemn face! Everything'll come right, sooner or later—and the devil take the hindermost!"

He was so gay, so absolutely his old, cheery self, that she could not help laughing back at him, and the next hour passed almost before she realized it. When he finally left her, she felt better, and had taken once again a surer grip over her emotions.

Anyway, she had found a true friend, and in these last weeks Diana had realized that few of her old male acquaintances had much use for her while she was unhappy and dismally unentertaining.

Dear Ronald—he was so nice, but to think of marrying him was so preposterous that she laughed at the mere thought.

There was only one person with whom she could contemplate marriage—and at the thought her smiles disappeared, and once again she re-read Sister Williams' letter.

Chapter 24

IT was the middle of November when Lady Stanlier tentatively approached her daughter, asking her a favour she would never have contemplated but for Diana's surprising consideration, which had lasted ever since their return from America.

It seemed that Lord Stanlier had accepted an invitation to shoot with his cousin, the Duke of Montderry.

Lady Stanlier was to have accompanied him, but her doctor was anxious that she should start a new electrical treatment against the neuritis which always attacked her when the cold weather arrived.

She was eager to obey his instructions, but at the same time, as she explained to Diana, Lord Stanlier hated staying away without her.

The visit was only to be for a week, and Lady

Stanlier was so worried that she braved asking Diana if she would take her place.

"I know it won't be exciting for you at Towerley, darling," she said apologetically. "Guy always has the same people, year after year, for his shooting-parties, but it would give Daddy so much pleasure, and I should be quite happy about him, if you were there."

Much to her surprise, Diana accepted, and a week later they started off, accompanied by the usual large amount of luggage, which seems so preposterously out of porportion to the length of a visit to the country.

Towerley was one of those country houses which have grown with every generation until it is a patchwork of three or four different periods. The front was Queen Anne, but two Georgian wings had been added later, and the kitchen quarters were ornately and uncomfortably Victorian.

The whole was surmounted by a dome of glass, which had been erected in the 'eighties by the last Duke, who was a very keen astronomer. It gave a strange expression to the house, appearing above the stone parapets and chimneys like a rakish bowler hat on a dignified old gentleman.

The many vicissitudes of building, however, had made the house the adored treasure-ground of children.

It was so perfect for hide-and-seek, so adventurous, with its many staircases and odd-shaped rooms, that once to use it for a playground was to compare all others unfavourably.

Diana had loved staying there as a child, but she had not been back for many years.

The Duke had grown old and crotchety, caring only for his pheasant-shooting, at least half of his life spent contemplating the sitting hens, or totalling and re-reading his many game books.

The Duchess played her part in country life with a perfection and dullness only attained by English duchesses.

She made the same speech over and over again at bazaars, charity concerts, British Legion fêtes, and boy-scout rallies. She accepted innumerable bouquets from tearful small girls in frilled muslin frocks.

She remembered, often inaccurately but nevertheless invariably, to inquire after the vicar's ailments, the doctor's children, and the mothers of the many district visitors.

The heir to the Dukedom, the Marquis of Wyman, was a disappointment to them. In reality, he was the second son, but the war had taken their best, as it had from so many other homes.

Gee Wyman had few brains and even less physique, and he had married, because he had been unable to withstand the determination of her mother, the plain daughter of a neighbouring landowner, who had developed since the marriage into a snob and a bridge addict.

Bridget Wyman was the first person Diana caught sight of as she and her father turned in at the lodge gates of Towerley.

"I was afraid," she said, "that Bridget would be here."

Lord Stanlier endorsed her sentiments with a little groan. He was fond of a game of bridge, but Lady Wyman's method of play, with the aftermath of disagreeable criticisms, spoilt his enjoyment, and, more than once, after his annual visit to Towerley, he had vowed he would never again play at the same table with her.

On their arrival at the front door, Bridget, who had been for a walk with the dogs, greeted Lord Stanlier effusively and gave Diana what she considered to be an appropriate welcome, consisting mostly of hearty innuendoes about the supposed gaiety in London.

"So you have torn yourself away from the world," she said, "to visit your poor country cousins! We must have a little talk later on, Diana, just you and I, and you shall tell me all the worst scandals you can remember."

She kept them waiting on the doorstep while she chattered on, and Lord Stanlier was relieved when he could escape into the house, to find the Duke awaiting him in the hall.

Diana took off her overcoat, gave her gloves and bag to her maid, and declared she was ready for tea at once.

The Duke led them, talking all the time of tomorrow's prospects of sport, to the drawing-room, where the Duchess awaited them.

There was a large group of people round the fire as Diana entered—oldish men in tweeds with pompous voices and pronounced stomachs; women, likewise clad in heavy homespun, with weatherbeaten complexions and hunting-field ejaculations, or primness personified, their lives of docile domesticity their only contribution to civilization.

Each and all were more or less of the same type, but one person stood out from them—one person whom Diana could not have missed, had he been surrounded by a million others—Ian.

For a moment everything swam before her eyes, and she had no idea what she said, or with whom she shook hands, until she came out of this dizziness to hear the Duchess say:

"Let me introduce Mr. Carstairs . . . Lady Diana Stanlier."

She felt Ian's hand touch hers and heard his grave.

"How-do-you-do?"

It was her father who broke in and interrupted with:

"Of course we know Ian—don't we, Diana? Haven't seen you for a long time, my lad. What do you mean by burying yourself on your outlandish island?"

And while this drew Ian's attention from herself, Diana sank gratefully on to the low chair which the

Duchess indicated, for her legs felt weak under her, and she knew that her hands were shaking.

Ian did not speak to her again, and she tried to force herself to attend to the conversation around her.

"Really, I have had to protest at last," the Duchess was saying. "I was as tactful as possible. I said: 'Canon, I have patronized this church for over thirty years, and I think six candles on the altar not only ostentatious but a waste of money at such a time. . . .'"

An old gentleman on her left, whose name she had not heard, was bellowing:

"Disgraceful—absolutely disgraceful! If the young fellow had been under me in 'ninety-nine he would have sung a different tune!"

Lady Ada Grantly had paused in her knitting . . . "red lips and dyed hair—I am never mistaken, Lucy, I assure you. . . ."

Lucy, the Dowager Lady Morgan, nodded.

"Just like poor Henry's wife—he would marry her, and of course the result was only what we all expected. . . ."

"Two hundred and fifty brace—that's not bad, eh, my boy?"

"No, sir. On Ronsa we think ourselves lucky to get fifty."

Oh, Ian—Ian! She could not bear this, and the moment tea was over Diana escaped to her bedroom. There she crouched down before the fire, which was burning none too happily, as is somehow invariably the case in large shooting-houses, and the room, without the comfortable central heating to which she was accustomed, was cold.

How could this have happened, she thought—but how could she possibly have anticipated that here, of all places, she would encounter the man she had so longed to see? Fate could not have chosen, she thought, a more incongruous place to bring Ian and her together again.

At Towerley they were both out of their element; both, whatever their differences, alike in the fact that they were vitally alive among this crowd of people who had never lived in anything but a peaceful backwater.

And yet she realized Ian would fit in with them far better than she. He at least was a sportsman, and therefore, as it were, belonged to that universal union which unites strange opposites, and waives class distinctions.

Now she thought about it, she remembered vaguely that she had heard her father talk of Colonel Carstairs being present at the Duke's shoots, and therefore, she supposed, his father being dead, the Duke had extended the coveted invitation of the first pheasant-shoot to his son.

Should she avoid Ian while they were here, or should she seek him out and strive for that interview of which she had been thwarted when he turned her from Ronsa?

Her mind was still not made up, and she was still uncertain of herself and her behaviour, when the dressing-bell rang. As she dressed, the question occurred and re-occurred in her mind, until she was more undecided than ever.

Of only one thing could she be absolutely sure, and that was that she loved Ian more than ever, and that she would do anything, even—she told herself, with a whimsical smile—walk round the world bare-footed, to have him once again in love with her.

All through dinner she was covertly watching him. She had no idea what she ate or drank, and the distinguished General who sat on one side of her, and the ex-Cabinet Minister on the other, were luckily too interested in a cross-conversation to find her not only dull but extremely stupid.

She was conscious only of Ian's voice, the attention he seemed to pay to Bridget Wyman, cackling inanities, or the charming courtesy with which he strove to interest the woman on his other side, who was slightly deaf.

With the exception of Gee Wyman, he was the youngest man present. All the rest were old enough to be his father, and Diana could not help noticing that the older men liked him, even inviting his opinion and listening while he gave it, and "my boy"-ing him, with the gracious patronage which is the privilege of the elder generation.

How proud she would have been, Diana thought, if only things had been different, and they had been there—as they might have been—as husband and wife!

It was in silent bitterness that she finished her dinner and sat through a weary half-hour with the ladies in the drawing-room before the men joined them.

The moment they appeared, Bridget collected together her bridge tables, and it was only after a lengthy argument that Diana was allowed to substantiate her inability to play, and also her disinclination.

However, at last she was excused, though not without some sarcastic regrets from Bridget that they could provide no jazz band or other night-club attractions at Towerley.

Six months ago Diana would have replied with spirit, and a repartee which would easily have defeated her cousin. But tonight she only smiled wearily, and as quickly as she could slipped away to her own room.

She did not go to bed, but sat gazing into the fire, her hands clasped round her knees. It must have been two hours later, when she rose to put more coal on the fire, that a knock at the door startled her.

"Come in," she said, wondering who it could be, and the door opened and admitted Ian.

She dropped the brass tongs with a little clatter, and turned to face him, her heart palpitating, her hands in a sudden hope fluttering as if to stop its wild beating.

"I am sorry if I startled you," Ian said, "but there is something I had to say to you, and I felt it was going to be difficult in this house to find a moment alone."

Diana sat down again in her chair. The face she lifted to him was strained, and her white fingers clasped and unclasped themselves nervously against the red velvet of her dress. Ian was in her bedroom, she thought wildly. . . .

How often had she watched him enter through her door, how often lain hating him, dreading the moment when he would touch her! Did he still want her? . . . Had he come to her again? . . . If he had . . .! If only he needed her. . . .

She felt breathless, and the blood rushed burningly to her cheeks. Yet when she looked at his grave, almost stern, expression, she felt chilled—she knew, before he spoke again, that it was no ardent lover who had sought her out.

He advanced to the fireplace, and stood there, not looking at her but over her head, his voice quiet, his words deliberate, as if he chose them with care.

"After you had left Ronsa," he said, "I realized how badly I behaved in sending you away like that when in the kindness of your heart you had returned to see me. No—don't speak," he said, as Diana made a movement, "let me finish. It is for me to tell you what I feel about the whole thing.

No man who has behaved as I have behaved to you can possibly express his regret in words, even if he realizes the enormity of his fault. I think now I must have been mad—in fact, I was mad—mad with rage, that you should treat me as you had.

But that excuses nothing. I could plead, perhaps, that life in the wilds had made me unfit for civilization —it has certainly not fitted me for contact with someone like you.

"My feeling about Jack you know, and the love I

had for you seemed to me the greatest thing that had ever happened in my life. But that again is no excuse.

As I convalesced at Ronsa, the full horror of what I had done came to me, and this past month I have been trying every day to find courage to write to you and ask you to see me just once, that I might strive to express the utter contempt I have for myself.

There is nothing more I can do, except to promise you that I will avoid any possibility of our meeting each other. All I pray is that you will forget me, and forget that such a place as Ronsa exists. I can never forget or forgive myself."

He finished speaking, and paused. Diana had dropped her head, so that her face was veiled from him. Then, as she did not speak, he walked towards the door.

"I would leave here tomorrow," he said, "but that might cause comment, which would make things even harder for you. We have only five days; and you can think of me as someone beneath your notice."

He said the last words with a bitter little smile on his mouth, and then, when there was still no reply from Diana, he opened the door and was gone as suddenly as he had come.

His footsteps died away outside, and there was the bang of a distant door, and then, slowly, Diana sank from the chair to the floor.

Her whole body was shaken by a storm of uncontrollable weeping.

Chapter 25

THE five succeeding days at Towerley were to Diana the most unbearable torture she had ever experienced.

She was acutely conscious of every movement Ian made, of every word he spoke, yet she was forced to act before him and the others as though she were utterly indifferent to him.

Every moment she felt as though she could stand it no longer, that she would tell him and tell them all that she loved him, and that, without him, life was utterly empty.

It seemed to her incredible that those around should have no suspicion of what was going on, even her father seemed unaware that she was experiencing any emotion other than a slight boredom with her surroundings.

The hours when they were out of doors, and she could watch the shooting, which was undoubtedly first-class, she could more or less tolerate.

But it was the evenings when her resistance was nearly worn down—when, after a long and dreary dinner, she would find it impossible to escape to bed, but would have to sit beside the Duchess while she knitted, or embroidered, listening through her incessant chatter for the one voice she wanted to hear.

Once she dared to ask the Duchess about Ian's father, and for a few minutes she succeeded in dragging her attention from the iniquities of the Canon with popish tendencies, and the stupidity of the local guide mistress.

"Colonel Carstairs was a charming man," the Duchess said. "Of course, selfish—but then most men are —but such good company, and an excellent shot. I remember Guy always considered him one of the best in England—I am talking of high pheasants, of course."

"And Ian's mother?" Diana questioned. "Did you know her?"

"Of course I did—her mother was one of my dearest friends. I can remember Edith Stanforth presenting her daughter in 'ninety-six, at one of the afternoon drawing-rooms. Alice was lovely, and she easily eclipsed the other debutantes.

I can see her now—she wore white satin, of course, and carried a bouquet of lilies of the valley. Even Guy, who was very particular in those days, thought her the prettiest girl he had seen for a long time. He told Edith so, and she was delighted.

Such a lot of nice men wanted to marry Alice that year. I remember, Lord Darwell was madly in love with her, but she wouldn't look at him, and my own nephew was broken-hearted when he was refused.

"Then Alice met George Carstairs—it was love at first sight for both of them, and luckily his father approved of her. He was very difficult, you know. Anyhow, they married and had eight blissful years of happiness before she died.

It was a terrible shock to everyone, it was so sudden —pleurisy. They were in Rome at the time, and before Edith could reach her it was too late.

"Dear Alice! So many people loved her, she was so sympathetic, so anxious that everyone with whom she came in contact should be as happy as she was. . . ." The Duchess sighed.

"Girls wait much longer these days," she continued. "Now you, Diana dear, must be twenty-five? . . . I thought I was right. I remember you being born—it was the autumn that Gee had whooping-cough, and upset all the shooting-parties. Guy was so furious, and we could do nothing. . . . Where was I?—oh yes, now I really think it is time you settled down, dear.

I know, you have such a gay time, and all that, but still it will end one day. Look at Maud Weston—she waited too long. And that pretty Jackson girl—Lady Jackson cried her eyes out when she refused Lord Bridgewater, but it was no use, and now, of course, I expect she's sorry. When are you going to make up your mind?"

"It isn't as easy as all that," Diana said. "I want to marry for love."

"We all want that," the Duchess answered, "but I always believe it is better to be unhappily married than not married at all."

"Oh no!" Diana exclaimed.

The Duchess smiled.

"All marriages seem to get to the same stage, sooner or later—the excitement goes, I suppose, and there are ups and downs. In our days we put up with both as best we could; nowadays, people scream for divorce at the first quarrel."

"I want to marry," Diana told herself that night. "I want to marry Ian."

How often she had scoffed at marriage, and despised her contemporaries who had been so anxious to find a husband, and to keep him. "Like cabbages," she had once described a friend who had settled in the country with her husband, leaving the gaiety of her former life without, apparently, a pang of remorse.

How right they had been, that devoted couple, to avoid the stupidity and temptations of London, where to be seen every night with one's husband was to make yourself an object of ridicule, and not to have an adoring cavalier was to own personal failure.

Once Diana remembered Ian asking her sarcastical-

216

ly, when she was pointing out several people of interest dancing together at the Embassy:

"Doesn't anybody in London care for their husband?"

And Diana, striving to be smart and cynical, had replied:

"Only somebody else's!"

How could she ever have thought such things not only amusing but inevitable? Loving Ian now as she did, she understood what a woman must feel when the affections of someone she cares for are stolen away.

Bad enough if the thief is sincere—but for a joke, a passing entertainment, that was unpardonable! Yet now Diana could recall herself saying scornfully: "Women who can't keep a man in love with them deserve all they get."

Her words, her actions, condemned her. She deserved to suffer. She had challenged Fate, and invited that suffering, and now she must bear it.

She longed for the days at Towerley to pass, and yet at the same time she could not bear the thought that after this she might never seen Ian again. He would never risk an encounter in London, and coincidence was not likely to throw them together in such circumstances as these.

It seemed so strange now when she looked at him, distant and preoccupied with things other than herself, to remember how intimate they had been.

"Perhaps," Diana reflected, "this is how one feels on encountering a discarded husband!"

But yet, she thought, how many better and more wonderful memories she would have had to keep her company had that been so.

Always with her now was the echo of Ian's voice, saying, "the love I *had* for you. . . ." The past tense! Everything that she wanted now seemed to have been hers in the past.

Without Ian, without his love, there was no future

for her, and she slept very little, lying wide-eyed in the darkness, her arms empty, her heart aching.

The last evening of the house-party arrived—they had stayed over the week-end, and the Monday morning would see the guests disperse.

Bridget Wyman could not resist just one more rubber—and then again, just another. The other tables had finished, and paid their dues, but Bridget, flushed with the only stimulant she enjoyed, refused to notice the advancing time.

The Duchess had long since retired to bed, but Diana felt restless and uninclined to seek the solitude of her bedroom, where she felt she had already spent too many miserable hours.

The men were taking refreshment from the decanters on the side table, and the other women were gossiping round the fire, mostly of their healthy horses and their ailing children.

Without saying good night, Diana slipped away from them. They did not notice her departure. Most of them disapproved of her, and the others found her dull, for they had nothing in common.

Diana walked up the wide stairs, climbing higher and higher until she reached the winding staircase which led to the tower. She had suddenly remembered that she had not visited it since her arrival—the quaint dome-shaped room had always thrilled her when she was a child.

It had been left unaltered since the former Duke died, the huge telescopes were still there, supported on great mahogany stands with adjustable heights controlled by a handle, like an old-fashioned camera.

The whole room was of glass, except the entrance on the north side and a low wall, about four feet high, on which the windows rested. This wall was hung with charts, some coloured, some merely drawn, of constellations.

Diana remembered that she and Gee, aged ten and

twelve respectively, had once damaged one, when scrapping for the privilege of using the telescopes, and both had been sent to bed before supper by an outraged governess. Gee had fasted, but Ellen had crept in to Diana with cake and hot milk, and had even read her to sleep.

Darling Ellen, Diana thought—but no wonder she had been spoilt! She had never been really punished in her life, until now.

She pulled open the baize door which had prevented the astronomer from being disturbed in his studies, and to her surprise a light shone through the curtains beyond.

She parted them, and stood suddenly still, pictured in her dress of white and silver against the deep-blue hangings, her cheeks flushed with a sudden lovely colour—for, standing in the room, was Ian.

"I didn't expect to find anyone here," Diana said lamely, and he held out a pipe with a smile.

"I thought this was the only place of safety to commit such an outrage," he said.

There was no strain in his manner, and she tried to answer him as easily, striving to overcome the paralysing embarrassment which made her want to rush quickly away.

He seemed to have altered. He was quieter, even older, in his manner. He had quite recovered from his accident, but Diana felt as though he had lost something which he had possessed before.

Vitality, perhaps—that tremendous magnetism which had emanated from him so powerfully that she had always been conscious of it, even if he were reading, or asleep.

He was not so alive, his virility was less obvious. Could his illness have caused this? Had she played Delilah, and killed his strength, besides the rest—or was it his natural reaction to herself?

"I loved this room so much as a child," she said,

"that I was afraid it would feel neglected if I forgot to visit it before I left."

She crossed the room and opened still wider one of the large curved windows.

It was not a very dark night, but a ground mist had risen from the river which obscured the view, encircling the trees, even curling tenderly round the shrubs and flowers in the garden beneath.

It gave one the impression of being perched high above the sea, and almost involuntarily Diana said:

"We might be at Ronsa!"

There was silence for a moment, then Ian knocked out his pipe against the window-ledge and replaced it in his pocket.

"Why did you come back?" he asked.

Diana hesitated.

"I heard of the accident," she said. "I was in the South of France when I read about it."

"But why did you come?" he persisted.

Again Diana hesitated. There seemed no answer save the true one to this question of his.

"I don't know," she answered at length, still gazing out of the window.

With a sudden return of the impetuous strength she knew so well, he put a hand on her shoulder and swung her round to face him.

"But I want to know," he said.

She avoided his eyes, dropping hers to look only at the pearl stud which gleamed in his white shirt, and as she did not speak he spoke for her.

"Was it an exaggerated sense of fair play?" he asked. "Feeling that, crippled, I was unable to fetch you back? Or was it because you wished to return?"

And yet she could not answer, for now the moment was upon her she felt suddenly terrified. He had spoken no word of love, not even in Ronsa, when he had held her night after night in his arms.

How could she tell him that she loved him, and

220

that while she loved him she was prepared to accept anything he chose to give her, and that was why she had returned to him?

But she could not escape now without answering, and while she swiftly turned over in her mind the possibility of every reply, he put his other hand under her chin, and tilted back her head, so that, whether she would or no, her eyes must meet his.

"Oh, Diana!" he said, and there was a sudden strange catch in his voice. "Can't you really tell me—or was there just no reason at all?"

"You turned me away," she replied defiantly, "when I wanted to tell you why I had come."

"I was afraid of pity," he said. "I knew I was ill, I didn't know how ill—but even if I were dying, I didn't want your charity."

He released her abruptly, and turned away, his chin set in the determined way she knew and loved so well.

"I am sorry," he said; "I am a fool to worry you. Let's hope for your sake we don't meet again. For it's no use, Diana—I can't pretend. I love you. . . . I've always loved you . . . and I'm not good at not getting what I want!"

Diana put out a hand to steady herself. He couldn't be saying this—she must be dreaming! But, before she could speak, Ian continued:

"I will go abroad—anyway, till you've married and have forgotten me. I shall go to Africa—and pray that I grow too old to care. . . ."

As if he could bear to say no more, he turned suddenly and strode towards the door, and would have gone had not Diana cried out.

Stopped in his stride, he had a momentary picture of her, trembling, yet her face radiant, her arms outstretched towards him . . . and then she was beside him, speaking, quickly, incoherently, her words falling over one another, her breath coming sobbingly. Yet the sense of it gradually came to him.

"I love you!" she was saying, "I love you! Oh, my darling—don't you see? . . . I love you so terribly. . . ."

Tears were running down her cheeks, but she did not mind them.

"That's what I came back to tell you . . . to ask you, on my knees if you wanted it, to take me back . . . as your mistress . . . as you would . . . I didn't care how . . . I love you so. . . ."

Suddenly the spell which had bound Ian gave way and he took her into his arms, crushing her so close that she could hardly breathe.

"Say that again!" he commanded. "My Diana, my wife, my darling—say that again!"

And with a heaven of happiness in her heart, her lips against his, and his arms around her, Diana whispered:

"I love . . . you, . . . Ian."